I0723126

GUARDIAN ANGELS

VOLUME 1

WILLIAM RICHARDS

STALKING P ART

WE ARE NOT DEFINED BY OUR HISTORY

CHAPTER 1
SMALL WORLD, BIG DREAMS

Ether—the lifeblood of all living things that roam the lands of Alterra. Mostly invisible to the naked eye, it flows through the air like wind and spans the vast water like a blanket. Over centuries, many have tried to study its unique power and wondered how it came to be, while others have focused their efforts on the best way to harness the source of creation for their own gain. Much is still unknown about ether and the potential consequences of its power, but what history does know is that all ether comes from a central location—the Celestial Realm.

If ether provides many mysteries with few answers, then for many, the Celestial Realm is little more than a myth. For others, however, it's a magical place so divine that they believe the ether flowing through it is nearly limitless. A realm that acts as the source of where all life came from, and where all life returned.

Legend says that the Celestial Realm is the land of the beginning. Those who were born with the planet were granted powers from the ether, giving them special abilities. These people are known as the Ancestors.

For centuries, theories about the Ancestors and how to reach the sacred realm swirled all across Alterra, but those who went searching were met with failure, or worse, death.

There are few people left with ties to the ancestral bloodline, and to meet one would be a miracle in itself.

But such difficulties never stopped people from searching.

However, there was one thread bringing both the Ancestors and the Celestial Realm together. It spread gloriously through Alterra, shaping its very way of life. That event was the birth of Angels.

Alterra was home to many different beings, none more complex in creation than Angels. Often known as the link between Alterra and the Celestial Realm, Angels were creatures born of pure ether, a bodily makeup those of ancestor blood were said to have. The other connection between the two were the abilities that made Angels truly special — their blessings.

Every Angel carried with them unique powers, unimaginable to the mere mortals who walked Alterra. Some came with incredible strength, able to level towns with ease. Others were blessed with outstanding capabilities to heal and protect the weak — and even those with the power to manipulate elements.

Through the years, however, such powers inevitably led to war. There were those who saw opportunity and would use Angels to rain destruction down upon Alterra, while others fought to defend it.

But those days were in the past. For 17-year-old Noah Andersen, they were nothing more than stories told in old history books. And history was not his forte. Noah chose to focus on the here and now.

The dirt crunched heavily under the weighty soles of his blue strapped boots. He kept a steady pace, the long, steel blade strapped to his back almost scraping the ground. There was no scabbard to protect the blade from dulling, but that was fine by him. He viewed each nick and dent resulting from battle as a reminder of his accomplishments.

He grinned, feeling the soft breeze rustle his mop of ash brown hair out of his face.

For someone his age, he was rather baby-faced. His teal eyes were round and youthful and carried the sparkle of an adolescent, a trait often lost when youths become older. But most people mistook him for a child because of his height. He was short. A fair bit shorter than others his age, and often even younger.

There was nobody around to dole out any mockery about his diminutive stature now, though. All that surrounded him were piles of rusted steel, broken machine parts, and mountains of what most would consider trash and clutter. The area's poor aesthetics were only matched by the strange odor that followed his path.

Of course, to most, that's all the small village of Berrios was seen as. Outside their confines, it was often referred to as the dumping ground of Alterra, not that the villagers had a say in the matter.

Except, in truth, Berrios was far from the area's dumping ground.

Alterra was a massive land split amongst miles of water that divided its various regions, and only Berrios had the misfortune of being in the shadows of an area whose people would treat it in such a disrespectful manner — the metropolis of Engvall.

Noah, if not all of Alterra, certainly knew of Engvall. It was regarded as the crown jewel of the Ekholm region and a testament to the city's self-importance.

Engvall towered over every other village within the region's borders, but this wasn't always so. Once upon a time, it too shared the same traits as its surroundings, comprised of small villages and run by a community that worked together to survive. But that all changed when one of the many mysteries surrounding ether was cracked.

Conner Engvall had long dreamt of a city run by ether. He was often thought of as delusional, wasting time, and neglecting his family, but he refused to concede. After decades, the visionary finally cracked the ultimate code of Alterra's greatest power source. And once he did, he learned to channel it into a tangible way of life.

From that day forward, the ways in which Alterra functioned would change. First, the monetary gains of such a feat were boundless. This would remain consistent in the Engvall bloodline to present day, but it also allowed for the once small village of Engvall to develop into a megacity.

Weapons and large-scale machines were all powered by ether, homes would no longer need torches as ether lamps could now light the way, and food became quick and efficient to produce. Even transportation grew rapidly. Thanks to the monorail system, people from Engvall could travel all over Ekholm, turning what used to be long and dangerous trips into fun adventures, if one could afford it. For those with access to such an incredible energy source, their dreams were limitless.

Although other metropolises would try to replicate the crown jewel of Engvall, people from around Alterra still came there in hopes of changing their lives. They could work in the factories, make a healthy living for their efforts, and provide for their families. Jobs were plentiful. Finding and mining ether, storing it, and condensing the power in such a way that it could be used without repercussions required nothing short of a full labour force.

History painted Conner Engvall in a shining light, but as the centuries passed, some began to view his lineage more grimly—in particular, the current heir to the Engvall fortune, Conner Engvall the Fourth. Some viewed his attempts at a monopoly on ether as a threat to the balance that made Alterra thrive, though few could oppose his desires, nor his resources.

Noah was born and raised in Berrios, and he could count the number of times he'd heard nice things about Connor Engvall the Fourth on one hand. To him, it had always felt as though people were being unnecessarily harsh, but he partly understood why. Since the self-appointed Emperor of his own city had taken full control of Engvall, life for the people of Berrios had gone from calm and peaceful to an enormous struggle.

Sure, some in Berrios had the privilege of working in Engvall, and they were appreciative for the opportunity, but those who weren't employed at the various ether plants were left to scrounge for money elsewhere.

There was no shortage of remedial jobs thanks to the growing population in Engvall, but they often paid poorly and filled up fast. And because Berrios was such a small village, there were limited chances to make a decent income. Some believed that Berrios would soon become unsustainable thanks to Engvall, and would shrivel out of existence. But Noah always believed those fears to be exaggerated.

Noah didn't work in those factories, nor was he doing well financially by any means. In a village struggling for funds, he was close to the bottom of that list. Thanks to his village's situation, however, he saw opportunity.

The biggest issue with Engvall's rapid population growth was how its waste increased exponentially along with it. Some of the scraps from construction could be re-purposed in the village for various projects, but much of the machinery that became obsolete or faulty would be tossed away like trash. And due to Berrios' close proximity, the residents felt that their outskirts were treated like a waste disposal. This display of arrogance had been a point of contention for years which only continued to worsen, but there was little the village could do. While Engvall's might was unparalleled, it was also so much more than that. Though sleazy to most, Engvall did provide a number of resources to the residents of Berrios — goods, food, and other supplies were delivered every few weeks, at prices most could barely afford. However, everyone knew that this was only a small peace offering to shut them up. If they were to dare spit in the face of Engvall, chances were they'd have a heavy price to pay. And so, for the time being at least, folks of Berrios endured what they deemed a necessary evil.

There was one good thing about Engvall's garbage, though. Each pile of trash, dirt, and scraps of metal formed walls that were generally around eight-feet tall that created a series of open-roof tunnels for people to walk through. The diameter was wide enough to allow merchant carts to travel between them, and it helped foreign visitors to maintain their path, as long as they could put up with the lingering stench of garbage.

For Noah, the wafting smell was just part of his everyday life. At first he struggled to battle the nausea that formed in his stomach, but now he didn't have time to waste groaning about odors. Besides, he spent more time than most in Engvall's "streets," and when the right mix of scents caught the air, he even considered the smell pleasant. Everyone else in Berrios was hard-pressed to agree.

Noah continued onward to his destination, the belts hanging off his hips providing a faint jingle. At the first intersection, he took a left until he hit a section of steel fencing.

He stopped and turned around, surveying the peaks and valleys of his surroundings. *Now where are those little scamps? I'm sure Uriel said they were at the edge of Dumpster Road. I wonder if they got inside again?*

By "Dumpster Road," he meant the pathways between Engvall and Berrios—an apt name for a place that featured mountains of trash.

But that description wasn't entirely accurate, as the paths between Engvall and Berrios were broken up into three sections.

There were the paths within the defined borders of Engvall Territory, which were far cleaner and monitored by the Engvall Empire. Then there was the middle ground, the most dangerous part on the combined path. It was known as the "Trash Pits," a large, fenced-off area that used to be part of Dumpster Road. After that was the actual Dumpster Road that led into Berrios.

The steel-linked fence in front of Noah stretched for miles. Even after all the time he'd spent walking in the Trash Pits, he was sure there were still small areas, new tunnels, and strange sights he had yet to discover.

The biggest difference—and the reason the Trash Pits were fenced off in the first place—was that it was often crawling with feral creatures, monsters that made travel difficult for those unfamiliar with a weapon. In other words, the merchants who brought supplies to Berrios.

Noah tapped the right pocket of his shorts and, not feeling what he was hoping for, reached in and pulled out a fluff of lint. *Come on*, he frowned. *I know I brought it with me.* He frantically checked every pocket in his shorts with no success. The lining of his green and teal coat, by chance? Nope. But in his top pocket, he heard a jingle and felt the rusted metal graze his fingertip. *Bingo—there it is.* He pulled out a small, silver key with three rusted chain links on the end. *We should really put this thing on a better chain. If I dropped it again, Uriel would lose her mind.*

The chain fencing shook as the wind rocked it back and forth melodically.

Noah gripped the key tight, pressing the defined grooves of the metal against his fingers. The simple padlock intertwined through the chain links on the fence might not have been the most high-end security measure, especially considering most of Engvall's other advanced technology, but that wasn't its intention. It was just a basic precaution to keep monsters in and easy fodder out.

He slid the key into the lock, gave it a turn, and then his magic wiggle to ensure that the often stubborn device would pop open. Once he heard the click, he pulled down and grinned. *Never fails.*

Before him stood jagged, rocky terrains with various tunnels and caves spread throughout, blending in seamlessly with the scraps of Engvall metal that littered every route. A less familiar traveler would struggle with so many different pathways between Berrios and Engvall, but aided by years of experience, Noah knew all the little tricks and shortcuts.

He ignored the caves nearby and headed to his right, his ears on high alert for the sounds of scurrying. He was on the hunt for trash rats, something he did often to make extra money.

Though the Trash Pits were surrounded by fencing and mountains of garbage, trash rats and other creatures would sometimes sneak in through the cracks. When they did, it caused all sorts of headaches for travelers, but especially merchants.

On a typical day, Engvall soldiers roamed the north entrance, while Berrios would be forced to guard the south. Anyone who wanted to pass through would need to be granted access by an Engvall soldier by way of a purchased ticket. Berrios didn't care to implement greedy policies like this, but since it was impossible to go from Berrios to Engvall without one, they were somewhat handcuffed to do so.

The reason that Noah traveled Dumpster Road and explored the Trash Pits wasn't to reach Engvall—he had no business with city life. Instead, he was on the hunt to clean up trash rats, even though it was actually the job of the Engvall soldiers. Along with manning the gates, they were also responsible to ensure safe passage, which meant patrolling the area and removing any infestation that cluttered the paths.

But most considered the Engvall Empire to be little more than an ill-suited army who sat on their asses all day, shirking any sort of responsibility that lay in their hands. Noah didn't like to think so poorly of an entire city, but some days those harsh notions were hard to argue with.

Besides, being on the bad side of anyone — or any *thing* — with the Engvall name on it, was ill-advised.

However, the Empire's slacking did make solid business for Noah. He was considered somewhat of a mercenary in Berrios, though by no means did he have an official title. Still, he happily took on odd jobs to help the village that raised him.

The most consistent job was always clearing the Trash Pits. Doing so helped merchants bring supplies into Berrios, and that kept things afloat — even with Engvall casting its shadow over them.

After a quick check of his surroundings, Noah kept on. His targets were rarely ever in caves, and so therefore he could narrow down his options. He pulled out a small book from his pocket and glanced it over. There were a few of his scribbled drawings, certainly nothing terribly artistic, but his notes were full of great information. He skimmed them over for a quick refresher and then nodded.

Trash rats, quite a bit larger than normal rats, generally liked more open, sunny areas where they could move around free of restriction. But their gruff, gray fur also made it easy to tell them apart from regular rodents, fur that spiked up on their backs like a porcupine's quills, though nowhere near as sharp. Their long, pink, twisted tails that dragged along the ground were also a dead give-away. Noah had never seen another creature in Alterra with such a unique tail.

Noah kept his eyes peeled, looking for trails in the dirt left behind by his prey, but there wasn't much activity at the moment. At first, he checked all the usual spots where they'd generally gather, but to his surprise, the paths were calm. He shrugged, undeterred by the minor setback and stuck to his routine. Because of the constant wind blowing through the pits, any trailing rat paths were swept away, and with them, any hopes of an easy task.

But Noah didn't mind doing a little bit of investigative exploring. He enjoyed the rays of sun, and getting some simple exercise in was always a good thing.

Up and down and back and forth, he patrolled for near-ly an hour but without yielding fruit. After 20 more min-utes of pointless exploring, he started to wonder if Uriel could've been mistaken, though it was rare that she didn't have her ducks in a row before sending Noah on a task.

It was unlikely but also possible that the Empire had actually cleaned out the trash rats first, beating Noah to it. Then again, Noah didn't really believe either of these theories. The request came straight from Uriel herself, and she was never wrong — or at least it always seemed that way. And the Empire doing work themselves when they knew that if they waited the morning out that Noah would do their work for them was highly unlikely.

After putting in a substantial amount of searching, Noah

stopped and tapped his chin, squinted his eyes, and tried to focus clearly. Most people in Noah's situation would turn back, call it a day, and collect their money without a second thought, but he refused such selfishness. If there were indeed trash rats banding about, he needed to find them. The consequences of him being wrong were too high. Merchants and other travelers could be left in perilous positions if he chose to take the lazy route, and having that live on his conscience wasn't a good idea.

After checking a few more areas, he caught a lingering smell in the air. Not the nauseating fumes of trash and scrap that had become synonymous with Berrios but a more pleasant aroma. Fresh fruit, perhaps? It was tough to tell, but it was a lead nonetheless.

Noah tracked the scent into a carved-out alcove, drawing his sword. He paused, his ears beginning to tingle. To his right, he could hear the sound of tails swiping and the growing chatter of gnawing teeth.

"Bingo," Noah whispered to himself. He passed through the tunnel and popped out the other side, still tracking the noise. When he reached the sunshine again, he finally saw his targets circling a handful of busted, wooden crates. At their feet was the source of the lingering smell—an array of fruits had spilled out of the crates, most of them smashed or half-eaten. "Not big on the table manners, are we? Uriel would not be pleased. Hopefully these were just crates that fell off a cart."

While the three, gnarly rats remained infatuated with their breakfast, Noah examined his surroundings. Not from fear of any ambushes—he could handle more rats coming out of the piles of trash—but to see if he could spot any merchants. These crates meant that a merchant must've been coming through the pits who could've been hurt, which would definitely take priority.

There was nobody in the immediate area, which supported his theory that the crates had popped off due to the bumpy road. The other option was that the merchants had made a run for it, which, when it came to trash rats, was nowhere near as difficult as one would think.

The spiked fur critters weren't exactly known for unprovoked attacks — particularly on Humans; they were far more interested in the food being transported. And they weren't picky about food either, which is why most experienced merchants travelled with spare scraps to keep the rats away.

Of course, those practices were now mostly frowned upon due to an unfortunate incident when one merchant ended up attracting an infestation of rats. Noah recalled the day well. It was his first and only time working with the Empire — the extra manpower was needed to clean up such a large mess. That said, with the excess of food scattered about and a scene that looked far from planned, Noah figured that it was a newer merchant.

Luckily, this job would be far easier than that day with the Empire.

Silently, he reached toward his hip and drew his blade, gripping the worn handle. There were small rivets along the edge of the blade, but unlike most nicks on the weapon, those were not by design. They were unnatural chips from wear and tear, and no amount of maintenance would be able to salvage it. But that wasn't cause for concern. He knew his trusty partner would hold up. It always did.

Noah held the blade's tip inches off the ground. If he managed to sneak up on the trio of rats, this job would be over in seconds.

But trash rats had strong hearing, and just one step forward would dispel Noah's hopes of success. At the first and faintest crunch of sand, he noticed the rats' long pink tails stop flailing. The rats pulled their attention away from the crates and focused on Noah, hissing and baring their sharp fangs. Their tails rapidly began slapping the ground, and the fur on their backs gradually began spiking upward as they prepared to defend their treasure.

Well, so much for that plan. Gramps always hated sneak attacks anyway. Noah charged forward, his sword low as sparks leapt off the ground. Not many foes were a match for Noah's speed, and trash rats were no exception. Before the rats could react, Noah was practically on top of them. He struck the first rat with an uppercut slash, and in one fluid motion spun around and swung his sword in a wide, circular arc.

The other two rats, seeing their companion take the first hit, leapt back and narrowly missed having the tuft of fur on their heads being shaved off.

One rat down.

The two remaining rodents snarled, their sharp talon claws digging into the brittle dirt as they readied for a charging strike.

Most people would describe Noah's sword style as unique and one that couldn't be copied. His feet were nimble and he always bobbed up and down slightly as he readied to attack. He was ready to move at the drop of a hat, which seemed completely illogical considering the massive sword he carried around with him. Such a heavy weapon could be viewed as a hindrance to his speed.

But for those who watched him, the sword Noah brandished seemed as light as a feather. He swung freely, always prepared to parry or defend incoming strikes in the process.

It was well known that this style was engrained in him by his grandfather, a man who'd spent years training him as a child. Noah was forced to hone his skills with such tough love from Gramps that some in Berrios even raised their concerns. But Noah didn't mind. He loved spending time with his grandfather, no matter what they were doing or how difficult things got. After all, it was always to help Noah prepare for his chosen future—a mercenary just like his Gramps.

Putting that training to use, Noah used his nimble feet to swiftly sidestep the torpedoing rat on his left. With rapid speed, Noah swung his sword and smacked it into the rat's tough underbelly. The rat sailed through the air, a nasty cut across its stomach as it crashed to the ground. Two down, one to go.

Behind him, he heard the scurrying of the final rat, who seemed ready to avenge its friends. Noah got in position and turned his massive sword into a shield. Using the blade's face, he absorbed the brunt of the rat's strength, but as he did he heard a strange crack. He glanced at his hilt for a moment, noticing a jarring crack running up the shaft. *Oh, that's not good.* Noah acted quickly, thrusting his sword into the dirt. The force sent the rat crashing into the ground, and before it could react Noah ripped the sword out and thrust forward. The rat used its razor teeth to chomp on the steel blade's tip, biting down with little success. Like a fish caught on the end of a line, Noah tossed the creature into the air before landing his final strike.

With all three rats defeated, silence once again returned to the Trash Pits.

But it wouldn't last, as he quickly heard an obnoxious growl. This was no monster, though. Noah rubbed his stomach, to keep the rumbles at bay. *Well, that was a good workout. I wonder if they left any food behind.*

He glanced around to ensure that no other creatures were lingering and then headed for the crates. Kicking over one of the lids, he took a peek inside and frowned. "Oh, come on—what kind of reward is this?" The crate was as empty as his belly, and all that remained were the undesirable leftovers from what the rats had been gnawing on. He was hungry, but nowhere near enough to ingest those dirt-covered scraps. He could wait until he returned to Berrios and got paid.

But one problem remained. Noah jammed his sword back into the dirt and knelt down to examine the handle. Running his finger along the crack, he contorted his face as he pulled on the metal. With little success, he sighed, "I wonder if Uriel can fix this? She's not going to be happy, though." He turned to his left and saw a nearby pile of scrap metal. Part of the scraps were hanging loose, and so he grabbed the nearest strip and dropped his body to the ground. The sound of screeching punished his ears, but he managed to peel the metal like a banana until it snapped off. He held it against his sword, eyeballing the fix he'd envisioned, and then smiled. "Yeah, this should work well."

After wrapping the metal around his waist for safe keeping, he pulled up his sword and reattached it to his back.

The trip back to Berrios was short enough, but the heat caused sweat to drip off the tips of Noah's hair. He wiped his face with his sleeve before shielding the beating sun from his eyes. *I swear it's getting hotter every day around here…I could use a cool tub right about now.*

When it came to exploring Berrios, there wasn't much to see. Pervasive dirt and sand, farmhouses on the outskirts, and some unmarked pathways with about two-dozen, scattered homes with no definable location planning. For travelers and merchants, there was also a small inn with three rooms, none of which were ever filled up at the same time. All in all, Berrios could be walked from one end to the other in 15 minutes flat.

The infrastructure was nothing compared to Engvall, but it also carried a much more personable feel within the trampled dirt roads. Kids ran back and forth laughing with glee, dirt smudged on their faces, their old clothes tattered. Adults had friendly conversations in the streets—there was no sense of fear and no security was needed. Everywhere Noah turned was a simple sight that made him smile. He loved his home.

Noah waved to a few of the children, giving them a cheerful grin which they returned in kind. As they disappeared down a side road, he continued along what most considered "main street," though that moniker was a modest description. At the end of the street was a rectangular building with scrap metal plastered on the walls like patchwork, a theme that ran throughout Berrios.

Since Engvall treated the town like a scrap yard, residents often made use of their free supplies. Taking the sheets of old scrap and using them to form houses, make signs, and even create tools that could be sold. The village was full of resourceful people.

Noah set his sights on the local store, which kept its doors open at all times. You couldn't miss it thanks to the scrap metal sign with the words *IZZY'S GENERAL STORE* spray painted in bright red.

He marched through the door and hollered, "Good morning, Izzy!" before turning down the only aisle in the store. There was no shortage of fruits, vegetables, and packaged meat resting on blocks of ice to choose from, but none of those things were of Noah's desire. He skirted past the "health section" and grabbed a pale blue bag of Spicy Sittler sticks. He had no clue where the name came from, but they were a delicacy straight out of Engvall. And every morning, he'd spend some of his hard-earned wages on those sticks, his favourite breakfast. He tossed the bag on the counter at the back of the store and dropped the key beside it.

Behind the counter was another door, and out walked a young woman with a blacksmith's apron around her waist, her fiery, red hair pulled back in a small ponytail. She grinned with the same youthful enthusiasm as Noah.

"Well, if it isn't Berrios' resident trash rat slayer," Izzy smirked. "How were those annoying scamps this morning? Hope there weren't too many roaming around." Her voice was warm and kind, but with a hint of curiosity, kind of like an older sister.

"Only the three, though they did manage to find a feast in some crates that fell off a merchant cart. But I took care of them, so we shouldn't have any trouble for the next day or two at least."

"Glad to hear it. Though I tell ya, those things have been getting braver and braver by the day. Soon they'll be marching right into Berrios if we're not careful."

"That's what you have me for," Noah grinned. "I'll keep this place clean of any trash rats."

"My knight in shining armour," Izzy said with a smile. She took a small sack of money out from the front pouch of her apron and tossed it on the counter next to the key. It jingled loudly as it landed, and then with a wink, "Breakfast is on the house this morning. Good work, kiddo."

"Wow, really? Thanks Izzy, but won't Uriel be mad at you for giving away free food?" Noah asked sincerely, perhaps even with naïve innocence.

Izzy picked up the Spicy Sittler sticks and looked them over. "Are you kidding me? These things taste like burnt mud—nobody but you would even bother going near them." She tossed the bag back at Noah.

Noah laughed, cracking open the bag. The sticks looked like regular potato chips, but incredibly thin and cherry red. He popped one into his open mouth and the loud crunch of his satisfying snack filled the room. He never understood why people hated them so much; they came with a kick of spice and tasted kind of like pretzels. Especially considering the sparse variety of choices he and everyone else had around town, he loved them.

Swallowing a few more sticks, Noah asked, "Speaking of Uriel, is she around? I need her help."

"Yeah, she's just in the back working on some equipment," Izzy said, gesturing to the back door. "Why, what's up? That piece of scrap you call a sword didn't finally break, did it?"

Noah shook his head. "No, not quite." He reached around his back and unhinged the blade, then laid it flat on the counter before pulling off the scrap he'd retrieved in the Trash Pits and placing it next to the hilt. "A trash rat decided to try and take a nibble on it. Luckily, the handle only cracked a bit. I think this scrap metal should be good enough to replace it."

Izzy ran her finger along the crack, feeling the depth of the groove. As far as nicks on a sword go, this was considered a crater. "Sweet Angel have mercy, Noah—that's a bit more than a crack. The thing's barely even functional," she sighed. "I'm not sure Uriel will be able to fix it this time."

"Of course she can! She's fixed much worse than this."

"That's really not the point." Izzy turned the sword upright and gave it a faint wiggle. Holding it parallel to her eye, she examined the blade before flipping it around to check the hilt. To the untrained, Noah's beloved weapon only showed basic wear and tear, but Izzy knew better. She could spot the subtle nuances of long-term decay. She pinched the blade just above the hilt and gave it a second wiggle. "This thing is weeks away from breaking completely. It feels like your blade is holding on by a thread." She returned the blade to the counter and turned around, facing a wall of basic swords behind her. Grazing over the selection, she plucked a similar-style sword off the wall. "Why don't you try one of these new swords I made? I can even give you a good price since you keep the Trash Pits clean so often."

Noah shook his head. "No thanks. You know that this

sword is my good luck charm. It lets me know that my grandpa is watching over me everywhere I go. He even said it was blessed by those way back from the beginning. It's never failed me before, and it isn't going to start any time soon."

Izzy stared at Noah with pleading eyes. This was serious. "Look, I know how much you love that sword, and I get how special it is, but if you're gonna be working as a mercenary you can't be taking risks with your equipment. What if it were to break halfway through a job? I'm only saying this because I don't want to see you get hurt. And neither would your grandpa."

Noah was used to this kind of counsel. Both Izzy and Uriel had tried to convince him of an upgrade for a while now, though never with success. Their sentiments came from a good place, but they could never understand just how much this simple weapon meant to him.

"Thanks, but no. I trust this blade. And I'm going to keep trusting it."

Izzy smiled weakly. "Suit yourself." She knew there was no convincing him to change and motioned to the door behind her. "Go on. See what Uriel can do for you."

Noah gathered his payment, grabbed his sword, and stepped around the counter toward the back room. There was a thin hallway with stone walls that echoed the sounds of heavy banging as he walked, so loud that he couldn't hear himself think.

He entered a much bigger room, with thin rays of light creeping in from the sky. There were slits in the metal roof that allowed smoke to filter through as the furnace continued to work, while also letting small beams of sunlight in.

The increase in temperature was drastic, and in seconds Noah felt the sweat dripping off his forehead.

Walls were covered with various suits of armour in different styles, and various racks held numerous weapons, ranging from swords to something that looked like a pendulum. As much as everyone in Berrios hated Engvall, a number of these weapons would soon be headed their way.

Noah located the sound of the banging, which boomed from the anvil in the center of the room. A tall woman was repeatedly hammering on a sword, its blade copper red from the heat. She wore an apron like Izzy, but also a welding mask as she bludgeoned the weapon. Her arms were bare but otherwise covered in strange markings and tattoos. Noah always wondered what they symbolized, but she'd refused to explain them.

"Hello, Uriel!" he shouted loudly as the blacksmith continued banging away. She reached for another tool on the rack next to her and kept working. It was evident she was almost done, which forced Noah to be patient and wait out the process. Though he knew little about the art of smithing, he'd learned through many firsthand experiences not to interrupt a master at work. Despite the seemingly violent act of weapon making, it was a delicate procedure and one Uriel took seriously.

Noah considered returning home and coming back later, but when he reached around and felt the jagged crack in his sword, he knew there was no time for delay. It needed treatment as soon as possible.

With one last dramatic bang, Uriel finally spun her hammer around and slid it into her apron. She lifted her mask up, its brim jetting outward like a ball cap as she admired her work.

Wiping the sweat off her brow, she asked, "It's quite the work of art. Don't you think, kid?" Her tone was full and powerful. "Someone of your talents could probably make good use of this thing—more than any of those Engvall army chumps could, that's for sure." She let out a hearty laugh without even turning to acknowledge Noah.

Noah grinned but shook his head. "You know I'd never accept a new sword."

Uriel picked up her work in progress with a pair of long, steel tongs. She examined the smoothness, and dipped it into a barrel before turning to face Noah. "Yeah, yeah, I know. But you're gonna have to let that hunk of scrap metal go at some point. It's falling apart at the hilt."

Noah sheepishly rubbed the back of his neck before reaching around his back. "Actually, that's sort of why I'm here." He revealed his sword as Uriel's face contorted in shock.

"Good lord, kid—I thought you were just taking down some trash rats, not fighting off the entire Engvall army. How the hell did you even manage to crack the entire hilt like that?"

Noah shrugged. "The trash rat got a lucky bite, I guess. I don't know…I didn't do anything different than usual."

Uriel grabbed the damaged sword and tossed it on her anvil before kneeling down to examine it. "Hate to say it, kid, but this had nothing to do with a rat bite. It was about to crack any day. If you're not careful, you're gonna be having lunch with the Guardian Angel."

"Damn…I really thought it would last a bit longer than that."

"Well, it might've if those lazy asses at the Engvall gate

actually did something. Of course, if they did any less work around the pits, they'd be a pile of bones."

Noah walked over to the anvil and placed the scrap metal beside the hilt of his sword. "For what it's worth, I pulled this from the Trash Pits. I merely eyeballed it, but I think it might be a good fit for the handle."

"Hmmm…it might work, but I doubt it'll be a permanent solution." Uriel wrapped the metal around the cracked hilt and started taking measurements. "Okay, this might work. Yeah, I can have it done by tomorrow."

"Thanks so much, Uriel," Noah grinned as he reached into his pocket for the bag of coins that Izzy had paid him, but Uriel stopped him.

"Keep the money, kid. The cost of ether is so high these days that you have to choose between having lights in your house or fixing your blade so that you can make a living. It's ridiculous." Uriel rolled her eyes, spat at the ground, and pulled her mask over her head. "But if I were you, I'd start wrapping your head around getting some new equipment. This thing won't last forever."

With a smile and a grateful bow Noah took off, leaving his precious weapon behind.

With nothing else to do, Noah decided to head home. Though not many actual streets existed in Berrios, there were a bunch of small homes that lined together like one would see in Engvall. The difference was in both the quality and layouts of the houses. Some had steps going up, and some others tunneled underground by a few feet, like underground ruins. Each was molded out of concrete with various chips and markings to signify their age — the more marks on the concrete, the more years the house had stood. All of them featured a boxy shape with a flat roof, although some folks used various scrap metal and other items to spruce up the walls.

Noah's house was one of the few that stood well above ground, with markings all over the front walls. It was the only home he ever knew, built by his grandpa when his family first came to Berrios.

He slid open the steel door, the resulting screech stinging his ears. Like the gates to the Trash Pits, it required some finessing, and even then it still scraped along the concrete floor, where there was an indented path from the trajectory of the door's movement. The door did, however, save him having to worry about people breaking in.

Noah stretched out his hand against the wall with the familiarity that came from thousands of repeated motions. His tap clicked a switch, which lit up a series of small canisters in the room with a pale, green light. This was the power of ether.

There wasn't much to look at inside, though admittedly the house was more decorated than most others. The walls were filled with different pictures, many from his childhood. Most were with his grandpa, and some with Izzy and Uriel as well. There were various towels scattered about on the floor which were intended to look like carpeting, but really, they just helped keep the place warm at night. He even had a couch and a TV, plus a small kitchen on the left side of the room. To the right were three doors, two leading to bedrooms and one to a bathroom.

A sense of comfort came with this familiarity, but Noah still stood in the doorway for a moment before walking in. The only home he knew was filled with all sorts of stuff from his grandpa's travels, and yet everything felt so empty.

He reached around his back to unhinge his sword, grabbing at the air before realizing his mistake. He sighed and kicked his boots off instead, tossing himself on the couch and staring at the wall toward two pictures from different periods. One was of Noah as a child, his youthful grandpa's arms wrapped around him, both beaming. The picture next to it was more recent. Noah looked his age in this one, and he was posing with the sword that was currently at Uriel's shop. Beside him was his now elderly grandpa, with a gruff beard and spiked hair. Even from the picture, the power radiating from Gramps was immense.

He sighed, slumping his shoulders comfortably on the couch. "It sure is quiet around here," he mumbled as his eyes closed. The room fell deafly silent.

CHAPTER 2
A CALL TO ADVENTURE

The air around Noah rippled as he swung his repaired sword with impunity.

"This feels incredible! It's even better than before. I don't know how you did it Uriel, but you're amazing."

The woosh that accompanied each strike was marvelous to hear. Each time his sword cut the wind, they could both feel the power in the breeze. His restored hilt sparkled like it had undergone a deep clean, and the chips in the blade were patched up with no indication of its wear and tear. It looked good as new, even if the weapon was nothing more than a mosaic of patchwork.

Still, Uriel gave a subtle smirk, basking in the glory of her achievement. Seeing the excitement on Noah's face was worth the effort.

Noah twirled the blade in his hands like he was fighting an invisible warrior. The rugged grip felt so strong that he could feel his full strength with each slash. Somehow it also felt lighter, more agile. He couldn't believe it. Satisfied, he stopped to admire the craftsmanship of the handle. It had been adjusted with his Trash Pit scrap metal to wrap around the hilt and cut in the shape of thin Angel wings.

"What's with the hilt being carved like that?" Noah asked.

"Seriously?" Izzy asked. Noah stared at her, puzzled.

Uriel plucked the blade from Noah and admired her work on the wings. They were more ancient-looking than common wings, almost like a stone relic. "They say that a pair of Angel wings is good luck from the Guardian Angel." She tossed it back to Noah. "Of course that could just be a bunch of garbage, but even so, I know your grandpa was a big believer in that Guardian Angel stuff, so I figured why not?"

"Oh. Well...thanks, Uriel."

Standing in Izzy's workshop, there was enough room for him to test his maneuvers and strikes with his prized possession, but he couldn't wait to get outside and put it to use.

Uriel crossed her arms. "I did what I could to polish it up, but fixing those chips won't last forever. If you're gonna be so stubborn as to keep using that thing, you'll need to start doing more regular maintenance."

"Yeah, I know." Noah groaned like an insolent child. He flipped his sword around, placing it on the table in front of him. He stared at it intently, each nick, each chip with its own story attached to it. "Grandpa used to tell me the same thing all the time," he nodded. "I just forget sometimes."

"You have the memory of a dead trash rat. Then again, your grandpa might've been more of the 'do as I say, not as I do' type."

"Huh?"

Uriel approached a rack of swords, pulling one out and examining her work. "The reason I have all these spare swords around is because your grandpa nearly shattered every blade I ever forged for him. He was a wise man, kid, and one hell of a warrior, but weapon maintenance was the furthest thing from his mind. That piece of scrap is the only thing he never managed to break. Granted, if he'd had a bit more time with it, I promise he would've found a way." Then, sharply: "So don't go breaking it, you hear me?"

Noah laughed off Uriel's serious tone. "Don't worry. You know this sword is the last memento I have of my grandpa. It's the most precious thing I own. I'd never let anything happen to it." He latched the sword to his back. "With it, I feel strong. I feel safe. It reminds me of the old days, like he's fighting right beside me the entire time. Telling me what to do, guiding my every move just the way he taught me. I don't know what I'd do without it."

Noah maintained his jubilant smile, a common feature for him, but there was no hiding the shift in his voice. It was always difficult when he spoke about his grandpa.

Uriel sighed and placed her hand on Noah's shoulder in a rare moment of motherly gentleness. "You miss him a lot, don't you?"

Noah nodded silently. He always struggled to find the words, and even when he did, he battled to use them coherently. "I do."

Uriel rubbed his back soothingly. "We all do. He was a good man. But he's with the Guardian Angel now, watching over this village. Watching over you."

To most people, Uriel was imposing—some would even say intimidating—and loaded with a short temper. But despite her hard persona, Noah was always able to bring out a different side of her to some degree. It wasn't just that Noah was so pure hearted—it was also because the fierce Berrios warrior known as Paul Andersen had spent decades working alongside Uriel as a mercenary. The two went way back, long before they'd stopped in Berrios. He was a warrior only defeated by father time, and one who was still highly respected. Paul Andersen was also Noah's grandfather.

Because of this, Uriel had known Noah since he was running around in cloth diapers, and there was a certain sense of kinship that came with watching him grow into such a fine warrior—one who was the spitting image of his grandfather. At least in a fight; their physical traits were actually quite opposite.

Uriel took a step back and let out a grizzled laugh. "But I tell you what, kid—if he could see you wielding that hunk of scrap metal around nowadays, he'd lose his mind. He hated any imperfections in his swords, even slight. Maybe that's why he broke so many of them." She picked up a wooden crate. "Anyway, it's time to get out of here. I've got supplies to fish through and I'm sure others around town could use your help today."

"All right—thanks again, Uriel."

Noah headed for the doorway but stopped abruptly, his ears perking up. Uriel glanced up as well, both of them focusing on the distant sound. It was obviously shouting, but it was impossible to make out any of the words. The two shared a concerned look and began hurrying to the storefront.

They spotted Izzy standing in the doorway "Izzy, what's going on?" Noah asked.

The young store owner's eyes were fixated down the street. "It's Engvall…" she said shakily.

Noah followed her line of sight and saw four men marching like robots down the main street. They were clad in green and black armour, thick as the walls in his home, guns strapped to their backs and swords at their sides. Their faces were covered with round helmets and black visors that shielded their eyes. Only their mouths were visible, but with no readable expressions. On the left side of their chest was a hexagon-shaped badge with a white eagle in the middle—the crest of Engvall. They couldn't believe their eyes—Engvall soldiers were marching down their street.

That in itself was a rare sight—Engvall soldiers weren't exactly well-liked in Berrios—but it was the two tall guys walking behind the group that really caught Noah's eyes. Although they looked moderately Human, their armor was quite different than of the usual Engvall garb. There were markings all over their bodies, and both had pale, blue skin. Their faces were also more defined, with bright, glowing eyes.

"Angels…those two guys are Angels," Uriel whispered to Noah.

"So that's what they look like," Noah whispered in kind, his mouth curiously agape. Everyone in Alterra, including him, knew that Angels were creatures of the ether, born of the Celestial Realm and sharing a connection with both those from the Ancestors as well as the Guardian Angel. But seeing them was not a common occurrence, at least not in Berrios. See, not many in Alterra were considered Angel worthy, and so nobody in Berrios had ever seen one — including Noah.

While he was focused on the Angels, the others in Berrios were flooding the streets, popping out of windows, and springing out from their underground homes to get a view. A visit from the Engvall army didn't happen very often. Noah could count on one hand the number of times he'd seen them step foot into his little village.

Most places in Alterra didn't welcome the Engvall army, but in Berrios the reception was particularly vitriolic. Residents would shout words of frustration, taunt them, and call them whatever nasty names they could think of — anything to get their point across about how they were treated.

In many ways, the whole spectacle disappointed Noah. He understood the frustrations with Engvall and the way the flourishing city treated his little village, but to direct that hatred toward people who likely didn't have much say on the issues seemed wrong. Nothing about their uniforms indicated that they were high-ranking soldiers — they were likely just rookie recruits chosen to be subjected to the fury so that more seasoned veterans wouldn't have to bother.

"What the hell are those filthy pigs doing here?" Uriel growled, her voice growing louder as she stood in front of Noah and Izzy. The sparks in her eyes were ferocious, her glare ready to stop the soldiers in their path.

"Don't know," Izzy responded. "I was just going through inventory when I heard a bunch of shouting from down the street. By the time I got outside, the circus was already in town."

Noah frowned. It wasn't that he had any sympathy for the Engvall Militia; they made their own choices and had to deal with the consequences. But the constant hurling of insults and threats painted his village in such a negative light. Seeing so many people he knew, people who treated those around them with such kindness, berating people in such an inhumane fashion was disgraceful. It was not the spirit of Berrios, and certainly not the way he was raised, even if their words were justified.

In three lines of two, the four soldiers and two Angels walked in trained unison. Each step was devoid of emotion, just fixated on moving forward to their destination. They refused to acknowledge the continual jeers being thrown their way, no doubt an incredible level of discipline.

Noah focused in on the two front soldiers. They tried to steel themselves from the anguish as any military member would, but Noah could see right through it—their lips were frowning, maybe even quivering. They wanted out of Berrios as much as Berrios wanted them out.

It soon became apparent that they were making their way to Izzy's shop. But it wasn't the sign, or the structure, or even the two women in aprons that they were focusing on. As they drew closer, Noah could finally see their eyes. The soldiers were focused on him.

As they moved in, Noah's heart skipped a beat. A palpable sense of danger abounded, like when wild animals stalk their prey. He watched the soldiers slowly reach around their back; the crowd's attention was rapt and both Uriel and Izzy closed off any path to Noah. But he shook off his fears and chose a different approach — he stepped between his friends and smiled.

"Hello there," Noah said with an air of innocence. There wasn't an immediate response as the front soldier, one of the two Angels, finished reaching around his back. Everyone was expecting him to draw his weapon, but instead he pulled out a parchment. It had the same seal that was stitched onto his armour and was tied with an elegant red ribbon.

Finally, the soldier spoke, his voice less hardened than most of the soldiers Noah came across when in the Trash Pits. "Would you be Noah Andersen?"

Noah nodded. "Yeah, that's me." He stuck his hand out but the soldier didn't reciprocate.

"You are hereby summoned for a visit to Engvall Tower, where you will speak with one Conner Engvall the Fourth. You are to arrive at Engvall Tower at noon tomorrow. All the information you need has been conveyed in this letter. I recommend that you be punctual, as Emperor Engvall is not a patient man." The soldier was going for intimidating, but the tone didn't fit his high-pitched, nervous voice.

Before Noah could take the letter, Uriel stepped in and snatched it from the soldier's hands, catching them by surprise. The others were ready to draw their weapons, and the Angel's feet twitched, ready to react. But Uriel was steadfast.

"Like hell! You can't just come marching up here and summon a kid to that tyrant's office. Have you guys no shame?"

"Yeah, what could a man like Engvall possibly want with a kid like Noah anyway?" Izzy added.

Both Uriel and Izzy were ready to draw their own weapons, but Noah waved them off, politely taking the paper from Uriel. "It's okay, guys—there's nothing to worry about. I'm sure it's no big deal. And besides, it could be a fun trip. I haven't been to Engvall since I was a baby, and I think it'd be cool to see how much the place has changed." He turned back to face the soldier. "You can tell Emperor Engvall I'll be there. Count on it." Noah gave the soldier a thumbs up, showing them the only sign of encouragement since arriving in Berrios.

But Izzy and Uriel were less than convinced.

"Noah, are you sure about this?" Izzy whispered.

Uriel agreed. "Yeah, kid—that Engvall is one greasy son of a slug. You'd better be on your toes if you're going to visit him, because only the Guardian Angel knows what the Emperor has in store for you."

The Angel soldier paid no mind to any of this and simply nodded at Noah. He turned heel and waved for his fellow soldiers and the other Angel to follow him.

This time as they retraced their steps, there were no boos or jeers—it was silent in the streets. Everyone was trying to process the terrifying request they'd just witnessed.

After the soldiers disappeared and the commotion settled for the morning, people returned to their daily routines. As for Noah, he held the letter in his hands, reading it over. He then shrugged with a smile and said, "I wonder why they needed a whole platoon just to deliver a single letter?" He looked back at Izzy and Uriel. "Doesn't that seem a bit weird to you guys?" They seemed unimpressed. "What's wrong?"

"You really are too optimistic for your own good sometimes," Izzy said.

"Oh, come on. Honestly, what's the worst that can happen?"

"Lots," Uriel interjected, intently focused on the issue. "There's something fishy about this. Emperor Engvall doesn't just send requests to meet with kids."

Noah's face fell. "Do you know something you're not telling me, Uriel?"

"Can't say I do, kid. Just the usual run-ins and rumors from merchants. But it seems pretty well-established that Engvall's dear Emperor is one greedy, selfish, arrogant man who'd burn his own family at the stake if it meant his own welfare would improve. He shouldn't be trusted. People like that can't be trusted. Now come on — let's get inside and see exactly what's in this summons letter." She headed back into the store, Noah and Izzy following close behind.

They gathered around the front counter and rolled out the parchment of paper. There was something strange about the eagle branded logo on the top; its eyes seemed to be moving, shifting around with each turn of Noah's head. It gave him chills.

At the bottom of the document was the handwritten signature of Emperor Conner Engvall the Fourth. In terms of official documentation, it was hard to imagine the summons as fake. That said, the letter itself didn't convey much information. If anything, it presented more mystery.

Izzy took the lead, reading the paper out loud. "Dear

Mr. Noah Andersen: This letter acts as an official summons to Engvall Tower to engage in a meeting with Emperor Conner Engvall the Fourth. We do hope that you will attend, as Emperor Engvall looks very forward to meeting you." The rest of the letter contained the date and location, but not much else. "Well that doesn't explain anything, does it?" Izzy said.

"Of course not," Uriel grumbled. "It's just a bunch of flowery language to hide whatever his true intentions are."

Noah, his optimism still unshaken, noticed a small, rectangular attachment at the bottom of the document—a thin, purple train ticket with fancy gold swirls on it. "Hey, they even paid for my ticket there—that was nice of them!" he said, peeling it off the letter.

"Noah, you need to focus," Izzy reprimanded. "This is serious."

"I know it is," he said calmly without looking away from the ticket. "But right now, there really isn't much I can do. Even if I wanted to, it's not like I could just say no."

"Sadly, the kid's right," Uriel started. "A direct summons request from the Emperor of Engvall is not to be ignored, not with what we've heard about that man's temper. If Noah ignored him, he'd probably be putting the whole village in danger."

Finally, Noah looked up. That statement caught his attention, and worry filled his eyes, which was rare for him. "You don't think he'd actually hurt all of Berrios, do you? All because I didn't show up? He can't be that cruel of a man, can he?"

Uriel furrowed her brow and focused on Noah, her tone sharp but clear. "Noah, listen to me very carefully.

You are not to put faith in that man. Anyone who has such a vast amount of power and control is dangerous. Unless you have that power, you can never understand the sinister lengths they'd go to just to keep it, even if that means letting innocent people get hurt along the way. So here's what you are going to do: You're going to meet the Emperor tomorrow. You'll listen to every word he says very carefully. When he asks you a question, you're to answer that question, nothing more. No going into stories about your childhood, or your grandpa, or anything else. While you're in that man's domain, treat everything as though you're under trial. Whatever you say could be weaponized against you, and we can't have that."

Noah frowned but nodded. "All right, I understand. If you're that sure the Emperor isn't to be trusted, then I'll make sure to say as little as I can."

"Good. Now wait here a second." Uriel stood up and made her way to the back room, leaving a confused Izzy and Noah behind. When she returned, she placed three, small round orbs on the table. One was bumble-bee yellow with a lightning bolt floating in the middle like an enshrined symbol, another a frosty, pale blue and white with a snowflake trapped inside, and the last a deep, crimson red with an ember suspended inside. "Take these with you. They don't have much juice left in them, but they could help you in a pinch if need be."

Noah reached for the snowflake orb while Izzy scooped up the ember one, each holding it to eye level.

There was no denying the beauty of the orbs — they had a translucent glow that captured light like a crystal. But they were far from simple decorations.

The heat radiating off the sphere filled Izzy's fingers with warmth before she quizzically looked back toward Uriel. "Excuse me, but where exactly have you been keeping ether orbs? Actually, better question: Why do you even have these things? They probably cost more than this entire shop."

"Took them off a dead merchant a few months back," Uriel said. "Since then, they've just been sitting on a shelf in storage. I had an idea of trying to forge a weapon mixed with their power, but that didn't go to plan and so I've got no use for them now. Better off with the kid than sitting around here collecting dust."

Izzy glared at the blacksmith, examining her face to try and figure out what she was talking about. Uriel refused to blink, keeping a perfect poker face. Her words were flat and to the point.

The suspicion was warranted, though. Ether orbs weren't something people just happened to stumble upon. And no merchant she'd ever come across had carried them.

There were a few reasons for this. First, ether orbs were the embodiment of pure ether, believed to have derived from a race long forgotten—the Ancestors. These were magical beings that channeled their powers through the use of the ether from the planet. There was little known about the Ancestors, and most of their history had been wiped away over time.

Over centuries and through thousands of hours of research, a way for mere mortals to manifest that magic came about. When ether was concentrated into its purest essence, it could be contained in a special orb. Holding such orbs would resonate with the ether flowing through a being's body, giving them the same basic powers as the Ancestors—casting bolts of lightning with the snap of a finger, using the flick of a wrist to toss balls of fire, and more. But due to their pure concentration, they were considered extremely dangerous weapons and painfully expensive to produce. Many regions, including Engvall and other military powers, would dig into the crux of Alterra searching for ether to create their weapons, also an expensive venture. Since the Engvall army were the only ones who could afford to produce these weapons in such great quantities, coupled with Uriel's disdain for anything Engvall-related, Izzy found it hard to believe they just fell into the blacksmith's possession. But she chose to accept Uriel's explanation and move on. There was no cracking that egg, no matter how hard she tried.

On the other hand, Noah shared no such suspicion. He was too busy examining how lightweight the orb was compared to what its size suggested. A power flowed through his arm, like a shocking tingle. It even tickled a bit.

"I've never held an ether orb before! They're so light." He gently tossed the orb up before an arm sprung forward and snatched it straight out of the air.

"These aren't some toys for you to play with. They're valuable sources of power," Uriel said, staring intently at the orb. "With these orbs in your possession, you'll be prepared for threats a sword could never hope to match. They're definitely a lifeline, but also extremely dangerous." She slammed the orb back on the table. "Now—I presume you know how to use these things?"

"I think so…grandpa showed me one a few years ago. He never actually let me try it, but I saw him use them a number of times. It seems easy enough, right?" He reached his hand out and Izzy surrendered her fire orb. Noah took in a deep breath as the warm sensation ran up his arm. He smiled as he recalled his grandpa's teachings.

He understood, in principle, how the orbs' power worked. It came from the ether stored in the orb, combined with the small amount of ether running within their bodies. But to explain things further than that was impossible. Even the most seasoned Engvall researchers didn't have a concrete answer as to why it worked that way. It was a melding of mind and body channeled through a medium of power that was the ether orb.

Noah gripped the orb like a baseball in his right hand, concentrating his mind on the sensation rushing through his arm. The tingle in his fingers felt like they were hovering over a fire but with no actual pain. With his free hand, he snapped his middle and index fingers together, and the orb lit up before sparks formed in the air above it. Like a flash of lightning, a small flame flickered into existence. It danced back and forth just inches above Noah's finger, no bigger than if he'd lit a match. That's all he desired for now, and knew that if he allowed more of his ether to absorb into the flame, it would grow to be a deadly weapon.

"That's pretty impressive for never having used an ether orb before," Izzy said. She grabbed the white, icy orb off the table, snapped her fingers, and a handful of small hail rocks formed in the air just like the flame moments earlier. "You just have to remember: ether orbs are just a medium that allows us to cast magic the way the Ancestors used to. But they still draw on our own surplus of ether as well — so just like ether orbs have a limit to how many uses they have, using too much at once will leave you fatigued."

Noah concentrated further, feeling the ether in his body heat up. His arm tingled as though needles were gradually poking into it, but as it did the flame grew bigger. The more Noah concentrated, he could feel the blood rushing through his body pumping ether into the flame. It made his vision blurry and he became a bit lightheaded — side effects that would be deadly in a battle. Or, in other words, the orbs carried some risk and reward to them. He closed his hand and extinguished the flame, and the tingling in his arm dissipated.

"Thanks, Uriel. But hopefully I won't need them. This is supposed to just be a meeting after all."

"I know, but better to be safe than sorry."

Just as Noah was about to depart, Uriel said, "Hold on, kid — before I forget, I've got something else for you, too." She disappeared into the back and returned with an elegantly carved wooden box that fit in the palm of her hand. She placed it on the table and pulled out a small key, using it to pop open the golden hinges.

"What is it?" Izzy asked, leaning in so she could get a better view.

Uriel pulled out a small chain necklace. At the base was a sophisticated stone carving of a cross, with something that looked like wings on the sides. A dull, unexciting gem was embedded in the middle.

"No clue. Your grandpa refused to tell me, but apparently he found it exploring ancient ruins when he was younger and then just held onto it forever."

"How come I never saw it?" Noah asked.

"Why are you asking me? It's not like I was the one who hid it. All I know is that right before he passed, he gave me the box and said to give it to you when the time was right, whatever the hell that's supposed to mean. Look, kid, I don't know what Engvall wants with you, but something tells me it's not going to just be for a chat. So take all the knowledge learned from over the years and listen to it. It'll serve you well."

Noah took the chain and put it on, cradling the end piece in his hands. "Thanks, Uriel. I will. I promise I'll be back soon, and I'll tell you guys all about what it's like in Engvall these days."

There was definitely some worry about what would be asked of Noah, but as he walked out the door waving to his friends, there was also a sense of comfort.

"That boy really doesn't see the bad in anything, does he?" Izzy marvelled.

"Nope," Uriel agreed. "And sometimes I'm not so sure that's a good thing."

CHAPTER 3
BRAND NEW WORLD

The sun was barely peeking over the piles of scrap lining Berrios as Noah walked down the silent street, admiring the pink in the sky. This was certainly nothing like when the soldiers were in town the day before. This morning, most everyone was tucked away in their homes, far from ready to start their day.

Admittedly, there was no real reason for Noah to be up and active so early. He was well ahead of schedule and could've even chosen to sleep longer, but there was a tangible excitement that kept him from lying in bed. The allure of Engvall had him twisting and turning all night long, not to mention all of Uriel's warnings.

And how could he not be curious? Uriel might've been harsh with her views of the Engvall leader, but she was right in one sense—people, especially kids, weren't just invited to Engvall Tower for a friendly chat. There was something tied to this visit. But unlike Izzy and Uriel, he was actually looking forward to finding out.

Noah had never met the Emperor, and so he knew he didn't have anything but hearsay to go on. But despite the warnings from Uriel, he wanted to judge for himself. It was only fair.

As he made way through the dirt-covered paths that approached the Engvall side of the pits, the air became cleaner. The smell was sweeter and lacked that certain, odorous trash-like scent. Everything felt so peaceful. He could just empty his thoughts and allow the day to come to him.

His belt was equipped with the ether orbs, though they were in casings to conceal them. Of course, his trusty blade remained at his side as well. It was uncommon to bring a weapon for a day trip to Engvall, but not completely unusual. Lots of mercenaries, or others known as holy swords; which were mercenaries that brought with them an Angel, made trips to Engvall. They were popular hires from Noah's understanding, but also cost a small fortune, depending on the job.

Noah worked his way through the Trash Pits and reached the gates that lead to Engvall, or at least the path to the train station that he'd take to enter Engvall. Luckily, there was no hassle when exiting the pits, only when entering, so the guards paid him no mind. Not that they would've done much — they looked barely awake.

After entering the Engvall side of the pits, he immediately saw that the trash was nearly non-existent. The fragrant aroma was intoxicating with plenty of flowers everywhere, and the dirt paths blended into sharp, mosaic-like tile patterns. It was like night and day. Perhaps that's why the people of Berrios were so frustrated — they easily saw what their village could look like if not for the city of Engvall looming over them.

Following the fenced path, Noah soon found himself in a simple, rounded plaza. Around the outside were lamps that flickered with the blue embers of ether, though they would soon shut off as the sun arched higher into the sky. At the east end was the train station and its many rails going off in different directions, but there were few other sights to see. Scattered about were some bulletin boards with various informational postings, a handful of benches, and a few different food carts that were currently closed.

Just off the north end of the ramps, which led to the different trains, was a booth with a man inside. It sort of looked like a jail cell, and the sad fellow inside did nothing to dispel that comparison.

He was young, maybe a bit older than Noah, but with a serious frown. Despite his age, the five o'clock shadow on his chin suggested he wasn't a morning person, which was cemented by the fluttering of his eyes every few seconds.

Noah approached the morose man and smiled. "Hello!" he hollered with chipper enthusiasm.

The man winced and said, "Take it down a notch, will ya kid? It's way too early for that noise."

Noah apologized in a much quieter tone, frowning.

"It's fine." The man sat upright behind the bars, trying to display some semblance of professionalism. "Anyway, it's a bit early for a kid to be riding the train, isn't it?" He stifled another yawn.

Though it was quite common for mercenaries and holy

swords to be riding trains at the crack of dawn, most were nowhere near as young as Noah—or as short. That in itself warranted a question or two.

Noah's charming smile returned to his face, though he made sure to keep his voice level. "I've got a long trip ahead of me. I'm on my way to Engvall Tower."

The man's eyes widened slightly, and then he raised a brow. All sleepiness in his demeanor was swiftly replaced with surprise. "Is that so?" He looked Noah up and down and saw nothing special physically, but when he noticed the black tarp wrapped around what was clearly the shape of a large sword, he said, "Aren't you a bit young to be a merc?"

"Beats me," Noah shrugged, handing over his ticket. "It's what I've always done. I don't think there's an age requirement to it."

The man wasn't easily convinced. He continued to examine Noah, gathering information to make a judgment call. Was he actually a merc? Was he hiding something? And, most importantly, was he a threat to any other passengers? Noah's cheerful voice seemingly refuted all three questions. Most mercs were grizzled and rough looking, and they spoke in deep, powerful voices.

Then again, what did he care? Noah had a ticket, and it wasn't this guy's job to decide who was allowed to ride the trains, just as long as they followed the rules.

"All right, go on through." The man ripped the bottom half of the ticket off and handed the top part to Noah. "Next train should be in about 15 minutes."

The train platform was a long, plain stretch of concrete with a thin strip of green paint streaking across the lip. In white letters, it said, STAND BACK repeated many times. There were also a half-dozen basic shelters that could hold at best five people at a time in the event of rain or snow, Noah assumed. Luckily the pleasant weather and lack of people around would make fitting into the shelters a non-issue.

Since nobody was around, Noah stood in thoughtful silence. He took a moment for his surroundings to sink in, admiring the vast valleys in the distance and the structure of Engvall Tower, though it was no more than a popsicle stick in the sky from where he stood.

Left with little to do but wait, Noah began to zone out. In a way, this was one of his best assets. He stood alone in silence, his head remaining empty. With no thoughts penetrating his mind, he could just wait and enjoy the moment. Most people, including his own grandpa, would marvel at how easily he was able to empty his mind. Then again, Uriel always claimed it was because there wasn't a lot in there to begin with.

The only sound that pierced this silence was the sudden blaring horn in the distance. Wheels screeched, sparks shot off in all directions, and puffs of smoke coughed out from the front of the vessel.

"Whoa—it's massive," Noah uttered under his breath. His ash brown hair swirled in the wind as the train whipped by him before coming to its eventual stop.

For all the great changes that ether brought to people's lives, the train between Engvall and its various stops across the region was life altering. Nobody ever envisioned travel being so simple and so fast while remaining safe. It was truly a miracle.

It was the first train that Noah could ever recall seeing, and he admired everything about it. The metal behemoth in front of him was coal black but sparkled with a metallic polish. Every few feet were green stripes matching the colours of Engvall. All 12 passenger cars had the words ENGVALL CITY EXPRESSWAY painted on them.

But that wasn't the only thing Noah noticed painted the train—it had been tagged with graphic graffiti. Images of an eagle attacking citizens, people crying out for help, rude words, and calls for an uprising. Noah contorted his face, wondering what this so called art, was implying.

"Are you gonna move, kid?"

The voice snapped Noah out of his trance and he noticed a tall man in a fine, black suit with a green tie. His hat had the same eagle symbol Noah was beginning to see everywhere.

"Oh, right. Um…yeah," Noah hastily replied. He handed the other half of his ticket to the man, who gave it a quick scan with a laser gun and stepped aside for Noah to proceed.

Trains were not something that most people in Berrios experienced, mostly because tickets were expensive, just like everything else created by Engvall. But to Noah's surprise, there was little glitz or glamour to show for the steep prices. Inside his car were two long benches stretching from end to end. The leather was ripped to shreds, and there was a pungent smell that put the Trash Pits to shame. The windows were grimy and looked like they'd never seen a day of cleaning. Along the top were rusty metal bars with thin loops that dropped down every few feet for when the seats were packed. This design made little sense to Noah, but he shrugged his shoulders and took a seat. In any event, the train was far from full.

Unhinging the sword from his back, he placed his keepsake weapon beside him. He tightened the string for good measure, which held the black cloth over his sword.

Even as an unofficial merc, one rule Noah did know was that in the interest of public comfort, all weapons were to be covered and or concealed. Any visibility of a weapon would be subject to Engvall discipline and confiscation. Sometimes this would be a fine, but other times a lot worse. Though strange in the beginning, it gradually became common practice and overall simply a kind gesture, especially to those who were potential clients.

Noah tried to peer out the window behind him, but its caked-on grime blurred any hopes of sightseeing. He decided to poke around the train and take in the new faces around him instead.

Unlike him, however, all the other passengers didn't seem very enthusiastic. Some had their headphones in while others buried their faces in local newspapers. But what stood out most to Noah was how none of them showed even a shred of happiness. It was the exact opposite of what he imagined people heading to Engvall to be like. All the reports on television and newspapers always mentioned Engvall as a booming city of opportunity and how great the lives of its citizens were. It was why he assumed that so many people in Berrios hated Engvall (other than the Trash Pits fiasco, of course). The robust capital was known as a utopia, and one that excluded the villagers of Berrios. His first impressions suggested otherwise, but he chalked it up to early-morning commuting and chose to let them ride in peace.

With around a two-hour train ride ahead of him, Noah started to wonder what lay over the horizon. What could the Emperor of Engvall possibly want with a local boy from a village he barely acknowledged? That was certainly not an everyday occurrence.

He could think of two reasons for the impromptu summons. One was fairly obvious: his skills as a merc were well known, at least in Berrios, so it wasn't impossible that maybe they were sizing him up as a candidate for the Engvall Empire. The problem with that option was that no matter how hard he tried, he couldn't imagine that word about his efforts in the Trash Pits had actually reached the Emperor of all people. Not without the help of some Engvall soldiers perhaps mentioning his name, anyway.

Noah did have some sort of relationship with the soldiers tasked with patrolling the Trash Pits. It was hard not to; after all, they'd crossed paths a number of times. But even so, it still seemed unlikely. First of all, he wasn't registered as a mercenary. There was a list of agents with proper channels to contact them, and even a card with their credentials. Some people even turned it into a full business.

Noah wasn't an *official* mercenary, but he did have a card—his grandpa's card, which he'd brought with him just in case.

Also, the work he did in the Trash Pits, along with fighting rats and occasionally dealing with other creatures, was just helping people around Berrios. More importantly, those jobs in themselves were not difficult. Any guard, soldier, or merc could handle them without issue, even the unregistered ones.

The Engvall army, on the other hand, were known for more drastic assignments than fighting off rats. At any moment, they could be called to battles the likes of which few in Alterra would ever experience. Killing other Humans and Angels, ravishing homes and towns…all the plights that came with the dirty jobs — jobs that Noah had no appetite for. Fighting monsters was a necessity, but killing Humans and going to war was not.

The second reason Noah could think of when it came to the Empire seemed like a stretch, but not necessarily impossible.

His grandpa had been an incredible merc and adventurer with a vast amount of knowledge. It always seemed like he knew all about the wonders of Alterra. People of Berrios even said it's where Noah got his curiosity from. Perhaps the Emperor was hoping to pick his brain about his grandfather. But if he was, the Emperor would be sorely disappointed — Noah didn't know a lot about his grandpa's adventures. For such a curious person, Gramps had kept a lot of secrets.

Noah placed his hands in his lap, locking his fingers together and releasing them repeatedly. He generally showed little in the way of nerves, but there was no ignoring the sense of anxiousness that accompanied this impromptu trip. Even amongst the thrills of seeing the big city and the honour of meeting with such a storied man, Uriel's warning couldn't simply be ignored. He'd need to remain on his toes, just as if he were fighting monsters in the Trash Pits. He could hardly wait, but he also wished there'd been more time to prepare.

That said, there wasn't much to prepare for without

knowing his reason for going there, so he decided to enact one of his grandpa's famous teachings. He rolled his shoulders back, taking a bellyful of air and gradually letting it out like a deflating balloon. Any slight anxiety he was feeling deflated right out of his body.

People often talked about Noah's grandfather as a storied warrior — a man who'd traveled the vast lands of Alterra in his younger years, meeting all sorts of different people and using his skills and strength to help them. In many ways, that's how Noah remembered him as well, but aside from being skilled with a sword, he was known for another defining trait, a trait he worked tirelessly to instill in his grandson as well. The art of mental fitness.

When it came to being a mercenary, Paul Andersen's arsenal was vast, but peace of mind was arguably his greatest asset. Being able to keep composed in any situation was key to being successful. As a merc, the chances of finding oneself in a precarious, if not outright dangerous, position at any moment was abundant, especially for the higher paying jobs. Those who were prone to panicking through rough waters would falter. And that could end in death.

But a warrior who could remain calm, flexible, and poised under even the most dire of circumstances could handle any situation thrown at them. All mercs worth their sword had the power and skill to fight their way through most situations, but many struggled long and hard to fortify their minds in ways that were necessary for true success.

In some respects, that's what made Noah unique from most — embracing mental fitness with ease. He rarely panicked, always let worries roll off his back like running water, and approached everything with a smile. Of course, that easygoing nature could be viewed as careless, and his trusting intentions were dangerous in a world filled with perils, but no matter how hard his grandpa tried, he never succeeded in giving his grandson a healthy dose of skepticism.

The tracks rattled loudly as the train ripped down the path. Every few minutes it would come to a stop, and a handful of people would join the ride. Still nowhere near enough to fill up the car, but it did make things a tad bit more welcoming, even though none of them showed any interest in Noah.

He glanced down and noticed the necklace under his chin, realizing he'd momentarily forgotten about it. It was an interesting gem, mostly because it contained so many mysteries. Where did his grandfather find it? And why did he hide it from everyone but Uriel for so long? There must've been some significance to it. Uriel talked about it being a keepsake from his grandpa, but Noah could never recall him being the sentimental type.

He tucked it back under his shirt. For now, none of those things were in his control. Whatever would be would just be—and anything else he could figure out as it came. He always did.

The rest of the trip went by without issue, and since the train was only half full, Noah could hear the screeching steel growing louder, along with the rhythmic chugging of another train—multiple trains, in fact. They were pulling into the station and when he glanced out the window, he realized just how far from Berrios he now was.

Unlike the single platform when he first got on the train, there were now more than ten of them, most with trains preparing for departure. Thousands of people were piling off and on like cattle — more people than Noah had ever seen in his life, and certainly more than Berrios could ever hold.

It was hard to compare the size of Engvall to anything he'd seen before. It toppled anything in the region of Ekholm, and surpassed all other kingdoms in Alterra, and when Noah stepped off the train he was in utter shock. One glimpse at his new surroundings exceeded any expectations he could've possibly had.

The train station was actually high up on a platform that circled the entire city, and when he stepped out to the Sky Bridge, he wondered if he was on another planet. There was no *way* this was Engvall, the city looming over Berrios. It wasn't possible.

Buildings were momentous towers that reached for the sky. Intersections and roadways were littered with cars, busses, and motorcycles heading off in all sorts of directions. It looked like chaos, but nobody was crashing into each other.

And the number of houses was astounding. They were nothing like the stone shacks of Berrios. A handful of the hundreds of homes Noah saw in one small cluster could've fit most, if not all, of the population of Berrios.

But one building rose above the rest in this city of standout sights. It was twice as tall as anything around it, with different plateaus every few floors and spiraling rings that circled it. It was also wider than most nearby factories. It could've been a city on its own.

The design was polished and sleek, truly an architectural masterpiece. And on each side of the building were the words ENGVALL CORP in large, gold lettering, which contrasted nicely with the mostly white exterior. Noah had zero doubt that this was the place he was headed.

Getting there, on the other hand, was still a question. Noah turned and noticed the crowd heading toward a few sets of stairs leading downward. There were also elevators that lead straight to the ground floor, but the lineup for them was packed. Never shying away from a little exercise, he followed the growing group and tried to blend into the sea of people.

Knocked and bumped like a pinball as he headed down the stairs, he did his best to keep pace with the crowd. It was shocking to think people would actually do this every day of their lives.

The sun was beaming when he stepped outside, and through the constant chatter of people coming and going he heard the train's horn ringing loudly. He glanced up behind him and saw the train taking off again from high above.

Up the streets he went, following the general direction toward Engvall Corp. For as big as the city was, it wasn't particularly tough to navigate. There was a straight path with a crowd following along it, which allowed him to keep pace.

He was focused on his destination, but becoming distracted wasn't difficult. There was so much to see, so many places to explore, so much he wanted to experience. Even though he'd arrived early, he thought it best to not veer off the beaten path and risk missing his meeting.

After half an hour of walking, his destination was in sight: the shadow of the towering building loomed from the other side of a wide, round plaza.

Noah noticed a gathering group near the front doors of Engvall Corp. They were on a grand stage with lots of lights and ether flares flying into the sky. *I wonder what's going on over there?*

His attention captured, he tried to wiggle his way to the front of the crowd. One of the few lucky things about being small was that he could fit his way through the thinnest openings. When he popped out the front, he noticed four Engvall citizens lined up horizontally, their backs facing Noah. A woman was approaching each person and speaking to them but Noah couldn't hear over the crowd.

Curious and with some time to spare, Noah glanced to his left and noticed a young woman glued to the spectacle.

"Excuse me, do you know what's going on?"

The woman pulled her eyes from the front and looked down at Noah. "What, are you new here? It's the unity ceremony."

"Unity ceremony?"

The woman finally pulled her attention away from the stage and gave him a confused stare. "You really *are* new here, aren't you?"

Noah nodded with a smile. "Yep, it's my first time in Engvall."

"Well, you're in for a treat then. The unity ceremony is where people get a chance to be blessed with their very own Angel. Usually it's those who want to join the army program, because if they can prove they can unite with an Angel then they're almost guaranteed entrance. Anyone can try, though. It only happens once every quarter, so you're pretty lucky to show up when you did."

"Oh wow, that sounds cool."

Noah's eyes grew with excitement. Not that he really understood what the woman was talking about, but the chance to see an Angel's birth was a sight not often seen—certainly not by people in Berrios.

On the stage hung different coloured spotlights that were dancing back and forth rhythmically. When they came to a stop, each of the four Engvall citizens onstage were bathed in a different hue. They turned around, took a bow to the audience, and then waved. Two of them were Humans, a man and a woman. Beside them were two shorter looking people with strangely shaped ears and small whiskers on their faces. Noah hadn't noticed before, but he now realized they were Ratataskers, a group much like Humans but with more fur and a fantastic sense of smell.

An Engvall soldier entered stage right carrying a wooden box under his arm, and he handed it to the woman who'd been talking to the contestants. From there, she cracked open the lid to reveal four stunning gemstones. They sparkled captivatingly like the ether orbs on Noah's belt but were nowhere near as round. In fact, they were all sorts of different shapes, like they'd been broken off the side of a cliff, with no discernible pattern.

The man on the left plucked the blue gemstone from the box and grasped it in his hands. The next three followed, picking their stones as well before turning back to face the stage. They displayed their hands forward to the crowd, cupping their chance at glory.

Another man, seemingly the host, walked onstage in

a lavish suit, his voice carrying though the excitement of the crowd.

"Hello, and welcome to our quarterly unity ceremony. The four of you on stage who've been selected by our gracious Emperor have been granted the great opportunity to attempt to reach unity with your soul stones. Good luck to all of you." The tone of his voice was almost condescending, as if he didn't believe that any of them would be successful.

Despite this, Noah chose to focus intently on the ceremony. It wasn't something he'd ever considered, but he found himself wondering what it would be like to have an Angel of his own. What would it look like, and what would its blessing be? He imagined it would be kind of cool having someone by his side at all times—if he could even achieve unity with a soul stone. It was something he'd never tried before.

The four participants stepped forward in unison, stretching their hands to the sky while holding their stones.

One by one, the stones began to glow brighter as though they were filling with energy, and soon the light began to bath their entire bodies, like they were in a trance or being possessed. Their bodies were glowing with white, but it wasn't as strong as the light from the stone—each person's light was flickering, struggling to hang on like a flame in the wind. When the light became less intense, Noah noticed the four people sweating. Their faces contorted in intense pain, their arms shaking as if the stones weighed a ton. Was it because of the stones' power? Could it really be that hard to unite with an Angel?

It was only a matter of time until the first man dropped

to his knees, his stone clanking off the ground and falling offstage. The stone's light faded while smoke rose from around it, and then a second participant fell backwards as though he'd fainted, leaving only two people standing.

"What's happening?" Noah whispered to himself. The woman beside him heard his question and said, "Not everyone can unite with a soul stone. They say that soul stones are a connection to the Guardian Angel. The stone communicates to the Guardian Angel to see if you're worthy of being bestowed upon the power of an Angel. Obviously, those two didn't make the cut."

A connection to the Guardian Angel? There was much intrigue in those words, and he wanted to ask more questions. But before he could, the light of the other stones became more concentrated, nearly enveloping the two remaining participants entirely.

The light expelled from their bodies, gradually morphing into figures. It took a few seconds, but when the light shattered, there were two more people standing next to the last remaining candidates.

One was a youngish creature, clad in thin armor that melded perfectly into its body. It held a long hammer with strange markings on its face. The second one was more Human looking, like a young boy, carrying two swords on both sides of his hips. For him, it would've been easy to blend in without anyone realizing he was an Angel, except for a few big differences — the same characteristics Noah had noticed from the army's Angels the day before. First, their eyes glimmered with a light that couldn't be hidden. They were enchanting. And, equally as interesting, the soul stones that were successful had morphed into a fancy ring. Noah immediately noticed that the ring was a match for the one their Angel was wearing.

Once the realization of success dawned on the crowd, they erupted in loud applause.

The two successful stone bearers were elated, through tired from their endeavor, but they greeted their Angels with exuberant smiles.

They were overjoyed with their accomplishment, but Noah kept his eyes focused on the two Angels. In contrast to their new partners, the Angels were not smiling, but nor were they angry. They looked…confused. But this made sense; they were essentially just birthed into the world and now they were being applauded and displayed like newborn puppies. Something like that seemed like it would be distressing for anyone.

Finally the young male Angel spoke, his spry voice matching his youthful features. "Hello, my name is Kapo. It is a pleasure to meet you." He took a bow—not toward the crowd but to the man who was now his new partner. In fact, the crowd might as well have been non-existent for the moment. The other Angel did the same, greeting the woman who'd brought it life.

Not long after, the crowd began to scatter. Some were heading to those who failed and tried to comfort them, while others were checking out the Angels and admiring the astonishing feat.

Noah wanted to join in the fun, but when he glanced up at the clock fixed on the tall tower, he realized that he needed to get a move on. He still had a meeting with Emperor Engvall, and that could simply not be missed.

CHAPTER 4
STRIKING A DEAL

The closer Noah got to Engvall Tower, the more he could feel his nerves creeping in. He'd been cool and collected previously, but butterflies were beginning to flutter throughout his stomach and his mind was racing with ideas. That in itself was rather unusual, so he chalked it up to a sign of excitement. At least, that's what he was hoping.

That said, he realized a level of caution was needed when talking to such a powerful person. Even Noah, the eternal optimist, understood this.

He tried to keep a positive outlook, but Uriel's voice echoed in his mind. She was so adamant about Engvall's dangers that he *had* to take them seriously — especially the threat of something happening to Berrios if he screwed up. That was an outcome he refused to let happen.

From the unity ceremony, it was a short walk for Noah

to reach his destination, and he stared up at the tower in awe as he arrived.

The monumental structure had looked grand from the train station, but up close it was almost unbelievable. The tower blotted out the sky entirely, casting an imposing shadow as far back as Noah could see. It could easily hold tens of thousands of people.

This begged a question in Noah's mind: why was such a tower even necessary? Was it all to bring the power of ether to people? Was it really such a difficult task that it required so much manpower? Or was there a chance that Emperor Engvall was working to unlock other secrets involving the use of ether? The more Noah wondered, he assumed the latter must be true. He wanted to ask someone, but he could hear Uriel's voice telling him to zip it. Now was not the time.

When Noah approached the imposing double glass doors, they split open, taking him by surprise. Inside, the first thing to strike him was the frenzied atmosphere. The loud chatter of those focused on work as they rushed from one end of the floor to another, the glamorous decor that spared no expense, the various places to sit, all packed with men and women in fancy clothing. Even the air itself gave off a scent of royalty. Had he walked into a palace? Maybe a shrine? And, if so, was it a shrine to the metropolis of Engvall or to the ego of the man who created it?

Amongst the many sights that caught Noah's attention, the one that amazed him the most was the lobby's glamorous water fountain. To have a water fountain *inside* of a building was unheard of by the people of Berrios' standards. Even more attention grabbing was the bigger-than-life gold statue rising out from the water. It depicted a tall, imposing man, stretching up about six floors. The statue wore suspenders and a top hat, which added even more height. Though Noah had never seen the Engvall family before, he figured it was of Conner Engvall the First, the founder of this incomprehensible city.

The first and most obvious course of action in Noah's mind was to figure out where he needed to go. He checked his jacket pocket, making sure he still had the invitation on him. There were so many people around to ask, but none of them showed any interest in helping him.

He intently surveyed the room like he was in battle before spotting a reception desk on the far side of the room. The waves of men and women dressed in their stuffy business clothes provided a tough challenge to maneuver, but he trudged forward attempting to break through.

People around here could really stand to be a little friendlier, Noah thought to himself. He continued like a fish swimming upstream, being bumped and hit multiple times on his wayward adventure to the desk.

After an arduous battle against the crowd, he could now see more clearly. There was an octagonal-shaped desk with an enormous amount of technology around it, things Noah didn't often get to see—computer screens, televisions, and countless phones being answered. He knew that Engvall was far more advanced than most other cities, but seeing it in person was jarring.

On the inside part of the octagonal booth were four people, all dressed in black and green uniforms. They somewhat resembled the uniforms of the Engvall army, but less bulky and more appropriate for everyday wear.

The quartet were talking to the others in line but Noah spotted one woman who looked the least busy and headed over. She reminded him of Izzy, though a fair bit older, with the same fiery red hair tied up in a bun.

"Hello there, how can I help you today?" the woman asked politely. She greeted Noah with a smile before noticing the elongated object covered in black cloth on his back. Before Noah could say a word, she knelt down, disappearing behind the concaved glass that blocked him from peering over the desk. When she lifted her head again, she smiled and said, "You must be Noah Andersen."

Attempting to hide his surprise, Noah returned her kind grin and nodded, "Yep, since the day I was born."

The woman grabbed a few scattered papers and popped open a side door from the desk. At first Noah was shocked by the woman's lofty height, but then noticed that the extra inches were thanks to a pair of lengthy high heels. When she walked, there was a clack from her heels that echoed off the tiles.

"Please, come with me. Emperor Engvall eagerly awaits your arrival." She gestured for Noah to follow as she began walking up a set of marble stairs.

Noah watched her closely with keen interest. Her disposition behind the desk was far kinder than those who were simply dialed into where they were heading, but when she walked, she carried the same air of authority about her. Was that the way everyone around Engvall walked? It was so different than what he was accustomed to.

Once at the top of the stairs, they reached three elevators. The one in the center and the one on the left looked normal, with glass walls creating the tunnel that reached upward. But the one on the right was different. It was black and green with the outline of an eagle on the door. The woman placed her ID card on the pad next to it, and after a pleasant hymn sounded, the door opened wide.

The adjacent hall was empty, much to Noah's surprise. Everything still looked as elegant and regal as the rest of the building, but things were far more private here. There were only a few doors on the sides of the halls, each with hand-crafted insignias on them.

Noah wondered what the rooms were for, but he didn't have time to ask before they stopped at the end of the next hall.

"You may take this elevator up to the top floor. There you will see Emperor Engvall's office at the end of the hall. He will be expecting your arrival." She crossed her arms and smiled, but instead of turning around and returning to where they'd come from, she chose to wait for Noah to enter. Was she just being courteous? No—it seemed like something else.

There was no debating that Noah liked to assume the best of people, but others often took that for a childish naivety. His senses were far from those of a child, though—years of practice allowed him to be quite in tune with when danger was a foot. And the woman's insistence when waiting for him to enter was definitely a red flag. Not that it mattered; it wasn't like he could just turn around and head home. That was the last thing he'd do.

But one way or another, he felt he was walking into some form of danger, so he took a deep breath and regained the calm mind he needed to move forward. He entered the elevator and turned around to wave good-bye to the woman, but before he could, the doors quickly slammed shut.

The eerie feeling from this forced Noah to reach for his blade, grabbing at the string that held the cloth tied around it. He stopped short of loosening it when he realized he was alone. There was no doubt drawing a weapon on his way to the Emperor's office would be the fastest way to die. There were probably guards everywhere.

He glanced over to the grandiose, golden E in elegant font that took up more than half the wall. Everywhere he looked, there was no mistaking that this was Emperor Engvall's building.

It was only a short elevator ride, but for Noah, time was moving incredibly slowly. There were so many thoughts playing on his mind, but for the time being, the only thing that mattered was talking to the Emperor. That way, he could understand why he of all people had been requested for this meeting and see what the great Emperor wanted. After that, he could go back to Berrios and discuss it with Uriel and Izzy.

The elevator came to an easy stop followed by a polite *ding* when the doors opened. Noah stepped into another hallway, this one much narrower and with a long, red carpet through the middle. On either side were vases with gold trim, each one more valuable than all of the stuff he owned combined. At the end of the hall was his destination, and it was impossible to miss. The door was absurdly large with carvings of a powerful man on each side, towering over those below him. The handles were nearly the size of a fully grown man and also made of pure gold.

There was no mistaking it—behind those doors was a descendant of the man who created the Engvall metropolis.

On the other side of the room was silence, which made Noah even more nervous. He would've appreciated some talking, some noise, something that made his circumstances seem normal.

He took one last look behind him, confirming that he was alone, but this brought up a bigger question. On the other side of the door was what most would consider one of *the* most powerful men in Alterra, if not the most powerful. And yet here Noah was, a deadly weapon strapped to his back and about to meet with him of his own free will. It was hard to believe that such a storied man wouldn't have a single guard blocking his doors.

Noah would never harm the Emperor, of course, but how could everyone else in the building be so sure? One wrong judgment call on their part and the Emperor could be killed. There had to be some form of hidden security in place.

He took a closer peek at the walls and noticed multiple small grooves, like tiny stabbings from a knife. Noah was tempted to run his finger across them but didn't—it seemed fair to assume they were security measures, but he had no intention of finding out.

He knocked on the door, waiting a beat to see if anyone would answer. Instead, the doors split down the middle menacingly, allowing Noah a glimpse inside. His amazement intensified as the doors slowly opened, leaving him standing in the entrance.

The Emperor's office was like a building of its own. There were two floors in the palace-like setting, the lower one featuring an elongated boardroom table with seats pulled out all around it. There was a miniature model of the city on the table, and on the far end a model of an unfamiliar area. Noah wondered if he was interrupting a meeting, but nobody was around to suggest that he had.

At least not on the first floor.

Noah heard a man clear his throat from above, and his eyes darted up to the second-floor balcony. That's when he spotted the Emperor for the first time. But it wasn't quite what he was expecting.

Staring down at him was a round man with fatty folds of skin on his neck. His burgundy suspenders were tied together with a black button-up shirt, the buttons looking fit to explode at any moment. He also appeared older than Noah had expected. He was clearly balding, and the thick lines under his eyes were visible even under his glasses.

Most would look at his physique and peg him as a fat cat tyrant who placed himself above everyone else, while also watching those beneath him continue to work for his benefit. And while that could be a fair argument, Noah noticed something different. He could see a man who'd sacrificed a lot for his dream—his health clearly being the biggest sacrifice of all.

He struck Noah as a man prepared for any situation, monitoring all sectors of the city every day. Perhaps it was so he wouldn't lose the power his family painstakingly gained or else be forced to watch his city crumble, but each wrinkle was another hard-earned step to maintaining the Empire he cherished so much.

The Emperor hauled his bloated body down the winding stairs before approaching Noah, extending his sausage-like hand for the young boy to shake it.

"Noah Andersen, I presume. It is nice to meet you. I am Conner Engvall the Fourth."

"Yes sir, I am. It's nice to meet you as well. This is quite the place you've built up here," Noah said awkwardly, unsure how to respond. There was no malice in the Emperor's tone, but Noah remained on edge.

However, being more astute than Noah gave him credit for, the Emperor picked up on his concern and said, "Please, Noah—you may relax. I promise to do you no harm." He withdrew his hand and lugged his body over to the far end of the table. "Please, have a seat. I'm sure you have many questions as to why I of all people would request your presence here. Allow me to first ask this: have you ever been to Engvall before?"

The Emperor took his rightful but enormous seat at the head of the table. Noah followed, selecting the spot closest to the Emperor.

"I was here once at a very young age, but I must admit that it certainly looks a lot different."

"Thank you. That is the goal for all of us here at Engvall Corp. We continue to strive to create the best possible lives for everyone who lives here in this magnificent city. All these people you see in this building, they are the ones who continue to push this city forward. They astound me every day with their creativity and ideas for a better tomorrow."

The Emperor's words were charming, which confused Noah more. Was everything Uriel said about the man false?

The Emperor asked a second question. "Tell me, do you know how this city was created?"

This was a question Noah could answer. He relaxed and said, "It's through the power of ether, the lifeblood of Alterra. From what I've seen, it powers everything in this city."

"You are correct. Ether is *everything* for us. It gives us life, brings us power, and allows us to achieve things only our wildest imaginations could come up with. In the days of my great grandfather, ether was first used to heal the sick. That's what sprung him to push its limits, leading us to the world we live in today. It is truly one of the greatest miracles our wonderful planet has to offer. Right up there with the existence of Angels and the evolution of man."

Emperor Engvall stood up and walked over to a cabinet just under the stairs to the second floor. From inside, he pulled out two thin tubes, one full of blue liquid and the other full of red. He returned and placed them on the table.

"This ether here takes over one year to produce in a way so that it can be used by our factories. Not only that, but the tubes you see in front of you are only enough to power this room for an hour."

"Only an hour?"

"Yes. Now multiply this over a year for my entire city. It takes an enormous amount of ether."

"I can only imagine," Noah said, fixated on the two tubes. Based on what he'd seen already in Engvall on this trip, he'd assumed it would take all the ether in Alterra to power the city.

"I don't mean to be rude, sir—but I still don't understand what any of this has to do with me?"

"You see, this life dependent on ether is something we have all become accustomed to. However, this way of life is not currently sustainable. As it stands, our ether consumptions surpass our supply by a significant amount. That is why I have requested you here."

Noah was rightfully confused. "I'm sorry, Mr. Emperor, but I can't say I know how to help you with that. I can't even begin to fathom where you would find that much ether."

Engvall laughed cordially. "No, I would expect not. And nor would I put the fate of my fair city in the hands of a single boy. That said, I do believe you are still of value. I have heard tales that you are quite the mercenary, trained by your grandfather Paul Andersen."

Noah kept his eyes on the Emperor, trying not to show his surprise. Still, he thought, *Did he know my grandpa? I thought grandpa hated Engvall as much as Uriel did? Am I wrong?*

But Emperor Engvall read Noah's thoughts and asked, "You're wondering how I know of your grandfather, aren't you?"

This time, Noah couldn't help but appear distressed. He nodded and said, "Yes, a bit..."

"I suppose he always was a quiet man. Allow me to fill you in. Believe it or not, your family actually has a long history of working with us Engvallians."

Emperor Engvall gestured to the 3D model in front of him—a scaled-down version of his city, and beside it was a stranger model, depicting what he could only assume were paths through a set of ruins. "These ruins you see in front of you are known as the Angel Island Ruins in the region of Kerfoot. I once hired your grandfather to do some work on the ether deposits there. He always did tremendous work in my efforts to make this fair city the greatest it could be."

"Wait, my grandpa worked for you? But—"

"You're thinking that your grandfather didn't like my Empire, and in a way, you are correct. We did have our disagreements, but Paul Andersen's work was renowned all across Alterra. His sword skills were one of a kind, and his wisdom and knowledge of the world were second to none. When I learned of that, I knew I needed him help to aid me. We eventually came to an agreement on how we could work together." The Emperor smiled. "How has the old man been lately? It's been years since I have seen him."

Noah stiffened up. "Actually, he disappeared a few years ago, unfortunately. And nobody has seen him since."

The Emperor stroked the stubble on his chin. "I see. I'm so sorry to hear that. Please allow me to move on to another subject then. The reason for this meeting is so that I may request your services. You are a skilled mercenary in your own right, trained by the very best, and that is exactly what I need."

Noah shied at the complement, saying, "I wouldn't exactly call myself the best. I've only ever done mercenary work for the people of Berrios, stuff like killing monsters and finding lost pets. I don't think that gives me any right to put myself in the same category as my grandpa."

Emperor Engvall grinned, emitting a hearty laugh that made his belly grow. Noah had an honest innocence about him, and it was something not beholden to most others the Emperor encountered.

"A modest one, too. I suppose I should expect no less from one such as yourself. If that is what you believe, then allow me to shed some light on the situation at hand. I trust that once you understand what I am asking, you will realize it is more than within your realm of capability."

Noah couldn't help but be intrigued.

"As mentioned, although magnificent, this city requires vast amounts of ether more rapidly than ever. That is why I have spent years deploying different groups from my army to scout out areas for large ether deposits. Doing so has yielded some fruit but also shed light on a number of dangers. The ruins where these ether deposits reside are swarming with beasts. We have lost many a warrior from what lurks below in the ruins."

"With all due respect, Emperor, if the army can't handle these beasts, what makes you think I can?"

"Because unlike my army, you have not let your talents deteriorate as a result of the peaceful times we have been blessed with. You see, the larger the army has grown, the lower the standards have fallen. I would dare say that at this moment, you're in the top ten percent of our soldiers, and that is exactly what we need."

"Really?"

"Yes. This is also why I created the unity ceremony a few years ago. Those who have the power to summon an Angel from a soul stone and unite their powers…*those* are the people I wish to incorporate into my army moving forward."

Noah leaned in, his eyes growing wider. "Does that mean you're giving me a soul stone to try and unite with?"

His eagerness made him forget who he was talking to for a moment. Uriel would've smacked him for that.

"Not quite," The Emperor said. "Soul stones are rare

and dangerous objects beholden to great power. I'm not yet ready to simply hand you one. But if you join my army as an independent mercenary and help our scouting team clear out these ruins on Angel Island, then you will have proven yourself worthy of a soul stone."

The Emperor reached into his back pocket and pulled out a transparent, white stone. The shining light reflecting off the stone was utterly enchanting. "This is a soul stone I have saved just for you. It will be yours—if this mission is a success."

"I…I don't know what to say, sir. This is incredible."

"I'm glad you think so. A team is being assembled now and I would like you to join right away."

Noah stared at the stone, then looked over at the model of the ruins. He had to admit that the thought of his own Angel was beyond enticing. He could already see the complete surprise on Izzy and Uriel's faces when he returned home.

But there was something else he wanted. Something that no Angel, no amount of money, and no negotiating could change his mind about.

Noah glanced down at his boots before placing his hands in his lap. He sheepishly grinned and said, "I appreciate the offer—I really do. My own Angel would be very special to me. But if you don't mind, sir, I actually have a different request as my compensation."

"Oh?" Mr. Engvall laughed, but he wasn't upset at Noah's refusal. It only made him more interested in such an honest boy. "Please, what is it you would request from me. Is it money you seek?"

Noah knew his desire, but the last thing he wanted

to do was offend the all-powerful leader of Engvall. He gulped and said, "Well…you see, sir…it actually involves my village, Berrios. With Engvall continuing to grow at the rate it is, Berrios has become a bit of dumping ground for all sorts of rusted metal and trash. It's piling so high that it's beginning to tower over us. I'll help you and the Engvall army, but only if you promise to clean up all the scraps and find somewhere else to dispose of it. Please let Berrios go back to being the beautiful green village it used to be."

Noah watched the Emperors face contort like he'd eaten something sour, and Noah feared he might've insulted him. But those were his terms for negotiation, and really the main reason he took the meeting in the first place. He wanted to help his village return to the way it once was.

Emperor Engvall stroked his bulging chin once again. He wasn't grimacing any longer, but his expression was hard to read. Noah prepared for the worst.

"First of all," the Emperor started, "I would like to give you and your village my sincerest apologies. Despite my attempts to keep a sharp eye on all aspects of this city and everything that pertains to it, I see that some issues have still managed to slip through the cracks. This appears to be one of those unfortunate cases. You have my word as the Emperor of Engvall that if you are to succeed in this mission, I will see to it personally that our construction teams clean up your village and remove every last piece of scrap that has been wrongly stored there. And, for good measure, you can still have the soul stone as well, since you've shown your selflessness in such an honorable proposal." The Emperor stood up, extending his hand once again.

Noah grinned, jumping out of his seat and shaking on their agreement. "You have a deal!"

Palpable excitement filled Noah to the brim, but he almost forgot the severity of the situation. Sure, a reward of gold would've been nice, but that would've only served himself. This way, he could do something for the entire village, a prospect that brought him more joy than any monetary reward ever could.

"I'm glad to hear it," the Emperor said. "I have high hopes for you, Noah. Your family has never let me down before, and I don't believe that you will begin now."

"This is great. I can't wait to go home and tell everyone the good news."

But the Emperor frowned upon hearing this. "I do apologize, but there is one thing that I forgot to mention. The ship to Angel Island will be leaving in just a few hours. There's no time to go home. However, I will send word informing them of the situation and that you are safe." He grabbed a piece of parchment and some ink. "Who shall I make this note out to?"

Noah felt stabbed with sadness. He realized that he wouldn't get to tell everyone himself, but he also knew that there was no going back now. He composed himself with a grin and said, "Izzy and Uriel. They'll be so glad to hear the news."

Emperor Engvall scribbled some words down and rose from his majestic chair. "Perfect. I will take care of this personally. And now we need to get you to the harbour immediately. The captain is not a fan of tardiness."

CHAPTER 5
A NEW ADDITION

Noah gawked. "This ship is massive!"

The tall, blue waves of the Seraph Sea crashed up along the base of the boat, and birds flew overhead like black specs in the sun. Fog horns sounded in the midst, acting as signals for incoming vessels.

He stood on the lip of a stone wall, peering over the Engvall South Harbour. There was one ship in particular that was at least half the size of Berrios. In a world of new experiences, seeing the vast water stretching across Alterra excited Noah like nothing else. Boats were one of the things his grandpa taught him about, and Noah was fascinated with the mysteries of the sea.

But the boats Noah had been taught about were nothing like what he was staring at. This boat had no sails, lacked the standard crew required to keep things steady, and was not designed with a lookout post. This was another product of ether — an ether-powered ship, capable of incredibly fast and innovated travel.

Only the south and east sides of Engvall were flanked by water, but Berrios was on the north side, so Noah himself didn't have much experience with the sea. And he'd certainly never been on a boat before.

The Seraph Sea was known as the body of water that connected everything in Alterra. There was always speculation about what could possibly live underneath its depths — treasure, forgotten lands, or even a possible connection to the Ancestors. However, exploring it was a task for only the bravest, and not something Noah was prepared to do.

When he walked down the steps onto the pier, his eyes remained glued to the closest ship. The metallic body with lines of green and yellow around the base were a striking monument to craftsmanship. The insignia of Engvall, the white Eagle, was also stamped on its side. Noah noticed two people on the upper deck making all sorts of gestures out to the sea.

Around the port were many different sites that accentuated just how different Engvall was from Berrios. There were groups of heavy machines driving around and picking up some smaller equipment before loading up the tanker of a boat.

Noah was unfamiliar with most Engvall army tech, but he knew tanks, jeeps, and artillery when he saw it. Combining that with the tense atmosphere around the army, he wondered just how big of a job this would be. If they were going to these lengths to deal with creatures in some far-off ether ruins, he would need to be on his toes at all times.

That was all right by him, though — he wouldn't have it any other way.

Before the Emperor ushered Noah to the port, he offered him the chance to peruse the Engvall weapons manufacturers to make sure he was prepared, but Noah politely declined. His own equipment made him feel comfortable. It allowed him to operate without fiddling around or feeling out of sorts. If what the Emperor claimed about their task was true, the last thing he needed was to risk distraction.

The pier was filled with pockets of people. Since Noah had yet to be informed of who he was working with, he decided to approach the group closest to him. After all, even if they were broken into different squads, they were all part of the same team. It only seemed right to get to know them.

With a friendly smile he waved. "Hey guys! I'm Noah — I'm new here."

But instead of being welcomed into the group, he was met with awkward stares. The army didn't appear nearly as interested in making friends as he was.

Not sure how to rebound from this, Noah prepared to explain himself but was interrupted by a far more imposing man than the others. The soldier, wearing a highly decorated Engvall uniform, had a number of gold badges on the left side of his chest. Strapped to his back were two mammoth axes laced with black and gold accents. His chin was chiseled and his face clean shaven with obvious battle scares. When Noah looked into his eyes, he could see an unmatched level of discipline.

Behind him, Noah noticed an equally imposing figure but with eyes of crimson red. And those eyes were unusually bright. He also didn't look like a typical Engvall soldier, nor did he wear the uniform of those around the pier.

Then it hit Noah: he was staring at an Angel.

"Hey, kid, you're not with the army. What are you doing here?" the decorated soldier asked menacingly. His voice was callous but it was his eyes, continuing to size Noah up, that made him uncomfortable. Every inch of his body was being judged and assessed for battle.

"Uh, hi—my name is Noah. I'm a hired merc at the request of Emperor Engvall. I'm supposed to be heading to Angel Island to help with an ether excavation mission in one of the ruins. But I haven't been assigned a squad yet."

"Ether excavation—" one of the men began to respond, but the leader cut him off.

"That's right...the Emperor *did* inform me that you were coming. You're with me, Engvall Gold battalion #227." The decorated veteran smirked, and in a flash he stepped forward and whipped out a small blade from his hip pocket and shoved it toward Noah.

Even the hardened group of soldiers jumped back, surprised by this action. But one of them remained ready despite the ambush. Noah gripped his sword, holding steadfast while the pressure of the man's blade held firm.

Horns locked like bulls, the man met Noah's intense gaze and broke into a wide smile. "Well, I'll be damned—that's some pretty good reflexes, kid. Maybe I can make some use of you after all." The man snapped his pocket blade back to his thigh and extended his hand. "The name's Bower. General of battalion 227. This here is my Angel, Crimson."

Crimson took a bow and said, "Please do not allow my master's actions to intimidate you. Welcome to the team."

Before accepting the gesture, Noah scanned Bower, looking for any indication of another ambush. The first instance he managed to act on reaction time alone, but only because of the distance between the two. This time he'd be in certain danger. However, Noah assessed the greeting as genuine and shook his hand.

"Noah Andersen. Merc."

"Well merc, come with me. We're gonna depart soon, and I need you on that ship with us." Bower turned on the heel of his steel-coloured boots and marched forward. His stride was powerful, and the strong air of authority surrounding him forced anyone in his path to step aside. As he headed for the boat, it acted as a signal for everyone else to fall in line.

Everyone began scrambling to pick up their pace. Meanwhile, Noah trailed behind Bower, getting the impression that he was someone who hated to repeat himself.

They climbed the oversized steel ramp onto the ship, which only left Noah more stunned. It was elegant, futuristic, and filled with many different kinds of people doing various jobs. It was like a small city was working on the ship in order to keep it running.

He recalled his grandfather telling him a story about being on a ship that could carry upwards of 100 people before, but this was ten times the size of that. Of course, he was learning that nothing the city of Engvall did was small. Or cheap, for that matter.

When they reached the front of the ship, Bower turned to Noah and reached into his pocket. Still on edge from the last test, Noah grabbed for his sword in defense, but Bower let out a low chuckle in return.

"Relax, kid." From his pocket, he pulled out two thin rectangular cards. "This is your meal card and room key. All meals are covered by the Emperor and must be paid for with this, so don't lose it or you'll be sleeping with an empty stomach." Bower let out a boisterous laugh. It was like his entire mood had changed after Noah proved himself worthy.

"There probably isn't too much else to cover 'til we actually get to the Kerfoot region. So strap in and get comfy—the waves are looking bumpy today. Wouldn't want you getting tossed overboard on us." He slapped Noah on the back, which nearly sent him tumbling. Bower laughed again and walked away to prepare for departure.

With Noah left to his own devices, he wondered what the region of Kerfoot—and more so, Angel Island— would be like. How different would it be than his home, and what would be the same? He hoped there'd be time to pick up a trinket or two for Izzy. She loved stuff like that.

In terms of Angel Island, Noah did know a little bit. It was said to have been named after certain Angels who used it as a base back in the Angel Wars. He also knew that it shared close proximity to the mainland in Kerfoot—in particular, a place known as Stone Cutter. Again, not a place Noah had ever seen, but one he recalled his grandpa mentioning before. Unlike Engvall, everything was said to have been carved out of stone. Perhaps he'd be given some time to visit the town when the job was over.

That brought up another question, though. How long was this job supposed to be? Would it be for the day, a week, or even a year? He hoped it wouldn't be that long; he wanted to see his friends again before then.

Even so, the thrill of a new adventure was getting his heart pumping. He was about to partake in the same kind of mission his grandpa would've participated in. Maybe he could even learn something he could teach Izzy and Uriel when he returned home. They'd be so proud of him. He glanced up to the sky and whispered, "Hope you're watching, Gramps."

With the ship on the verge of departing, Noah headed to the bow and peered over the edge. The angular shape of the bow continued to cut the waves despite still being tied to the dock. Noah's eyes shimmered with the same sparkles of the crystal water rippling before him. It was magical, and the sounds of the waves gently rocking up against the boat gave him a soothing song to hum to himself.

After a few moments of silence, Noah heard Bower's booming voice piercing his tranquility over the loudspeaker. The leader of Battalion 227 said, "Listen up, lot. We're loaded up and ready to depart for Angel Island. Food is in the mess hall on the second deck, and beds are on the lower deck. Fill your bellies and get some rest. We have a long day of travel ahead of us."

A bellowing horn signaled their departure, and all of the soldiers on the lower decks started to mobilize, creating a racket from all the commotion.

Noah watched them trickle in, leaving their machines and other operations as they went off to grab some grub. Noah was hungry too, and his stomach was fighting with him to join them. But before he did, he wanted to watch the ship set sail first. That, too, was a new experience he really wished to see.

The horn began to sound in intervals, and gradually the boat began to sway. It took a moment to fire up the engines and get things into full gear.

Noah returned to leaning over the deck, watching as his homeland began to fade into the distance.

He admired the sea for a few minutes, looking out at the entire world before him. He smiled with his head in his hands. *I'm really doing this. I wonder what Uriel and Izzy are thinking right now? They'd probably tell me to make sure I eat.* His stomach let out an empty grumble. *Well, better listen to them, I guess.*

Noah wasn't sure what to expect from the mess hall, but he was pleasantly surprised regardless. He'd imagined it to be cramped, musty, and filled with all sorts of mysterious, concerning smells. But, as he was learning, everything related to Engvall was of the highest quality.

There were chandeliers hanging from the ceiling and about 100 round tables that sat six to ten people each, decorated in elegant white table cloths like they were in a royal cruise ship. In the back row were different booths with various lineups of soldiers, grabbing trays and being served food from each of the booths. Every few seconds someone else, usually dressed like a chef, would pop out from the door behind the booths to bring more food.

One had to wonder if the soldiers really cared for such glitz and glam; some were eating like barbarians and stuffing down everything in sight, while others were playing card games and even arm wrestling. It was two polar opposites from those in the trenches compared to those sitting cushy in Engvall Tower.

But Noah cared more about the food than the hall's appearance. And based on the intoxicating smell filling the hall, he knew he was in for a treat.

He was also excited to meet some of his fellow soldiers.

There was no debating the Engvall army's reputation in Berrios, but that always seemed unfair to Noah. They were people just like him. They had families, dreams, and fears—things that friends could bond over. And with any luck, maybe he could smooth over any tension.

Unfortunately, not everyone was as receptive to Noah as he was to them. He picked the table closest to him and approached it with his usually infectious smile. There were a group of five men and one woman, all with their helmets off and placed on the table. They were also rather large Humans, especially compared to Noah, with buff muscles and hardened expressions.

He got closer and waved to the table, but nobody turned their head. They were locked in on the card game taking place, tossing pieces of silver and gold onto the table as they drew cards.

Noah tried again. "Hey, guys—whatcha playing?" This time, he caught the groups attention but not their interest. He could feel it once again, a group of eyes sizing him up and deciding whether to take the bait.

The seconds were agonizingly long, but eventually the group turned their attention back to the game. The one closest to Noah said, "Sorry, merc—we're full," in a tone that could freeze the water they were coasting on.

Sure, Noah wanted to make friends, but he also knew

when not to stick his nose into things, and this was definitely one of those times. He wisely chose to walk away and headed for another table.

Except it was more of the same everywhere he went. Nobody wanted to go near him, and he didn't understand why. Was it because he was a merc? Sure he wasn't a real member of the army, but they were all working toward the same goal in the end. He thought perhaps it had to do with his age; so far, everyone around the ship were a fair bit older than him. That seemed unlikely though, since their ages varied as well. The last option was that maybe they viewed him as a threat—not in terms of violence but regarding job security. Emperor Engvall had made it clear that he was bringing in mercs due to falling standards, which was certainly an insult to any soldier's pride.

Though his appetite started to wane, Noah grabbed some food and did his best to avoid potential issues. Since he had nobody to eat with, he decided to take his meal and head back out to the bottom deck. At least he could listen to the waves instead of eating in silence.

After finishing his meal, which should've been a delight but wasn't due to his loneliness, Noah decided to take a walk around the deck. Most people remained in the mess hall, which made noticing the only other soldier leaning over the edge of the boat far easier. A fellow merc outcast, perhaps?

Noah wandered on over, but the closer he got, he realized that the man's head was dipping down over the rail. The soldier started making unsavory gagging sounds.

Noah hurried to the man, whose head was still hanging overboard, when they hit a heavy wave. The boat shook and dipped to the left, causing the soldier's feet to leave the deck as momentum carried him into the air. He looked as though he was about to let out a scream unfitting of an army member before coming to a sudden stop. He dangled over the side of the boat, all of the blood rushing to his head, and anything left in his stomach was heaved into the sea.

Noah wrapped his body around the man's legs and dropped his weight, saying though gritted teeth, "I got you! Just hang on..." Noah started using all his strength to pull the man up, praying the ship didn't bounce them both overboard from another heavy wave.

One violent heave ripped the soldier over the railing and back onto the deck. He crashed down on his back, his chest gasping for air.

"I hate the sea," the man groaned. It seemed like the sounds of the ocean were making his stomach queasy, but he managed.

Noah got to his knees and peered over the man's body. His face was still pale and covered in sweat. Gradually, the man's eyes opened and he met Noah's concerned frown with a look of mental anguish.

"That was a close one. Are you all right?" Noah asked, shifting his worried face to a more comforting smile. He reached his hand down to help the man up, but was shaken off. But this time it wasn't out of rudeness.

"Actually, if you don't mind, I think I'm just gonna lay here for a few minutes," the soldier said through heavy breaths. "It's probably safer that way."

Noah laughed a little and said, "Okay, well do you mind if I sit next to you then?" The seasick soldier detected sincerity in Noah's voice, which softened him.

The soldier lifted his head slightly to look at his saviour, then dropped again and grimaced, "Uh…yeah, sure. Whatever…as long as I don't have to get up, you can do what you want." He half-seated himself before leaning back against the wall of the ship deck. His face was turning a nauseous green, but his sweating began to subside. Noah joined him, and the two glanced up as the sun began setting on the horizon.

The man burped and then tilted his head, noticing Noah's lack of uniform. "You're not part of the army, are you?"

"Uh…not quite. I'm a bit of a part timer."

"A hired merc from the Emperor, you mean?"

Noah prepared to respond but the man continued. "Look a bit young if you ask me, but whatever. You got a name, kid?"

"Yeah, it's Noah."

"Well, Noah, I owe you one. The names Garrett, but everyone around her calls me Frost."

"Frost?" Noah asked. His voice sounded more intrigued than was common for an army guy.

"Yeah, not the most creative name, but then again, soldiers aren't known for being clever. They gave me the name 'cause whereas everyone else likes their swords or their guns, I'm a pro with *these*." Frost unclipped a few casings from his belt and dumped out three orbs.

"Whoa," Noah marvelled, "that's like a small fortune of ether orbs." Each of the orbs cast off a breath of freezing air, and shined in a pale blue and white.

"Ah, I see you've got some experience with ether orbs then."

Noah shook his head. "Honestly, not quite. I have a few different ones, but I've never used them. They were just gifted to me for this trip." Noah popped open his own casings around his belt and pulled out his orbs, placing them beside Frost's.

"Damn, kid. Whoever gave you these didn't leave you with much, did they?" Frost picked up Noah's ice orb and gave it a once over. "Look at the colour on this thing. It's practically lost all its ether." He grabbed his own orb. "Here, take this one—chances are it'll actually help you in a pinch." He swapped the orbs and handed Noah the powerfully glowing one.

"Wait, really? Are you sure? Don't you need it for the mission?"

Frost shrugged. "Consider it payment for saving me from going overboard. And besides, I'm not big on getting my hands dirty if I don't have to. I like to let the heavy guns deal with that stuff." He tried to laugh, but then a wave of nausea hit him. He grabbed his stomach and groaned before slumping further.

"So, what're you doing out here, anyway? Figured a merc would be scarfing down free food and trying to swindle us soldiers out of our paychecks."

"What?" Noah gawked.

Frost laughed. "Never mind, maybe those are just rumours."

Noah pressed his legs into his chest, and for a moment he didn't resemble a warrior but rather a child, and one who had little in the way of friends and family. "Honestly, it seems like none of the other soldiers are too happy with me being here. I tried to talk to others in the mess hall, but they just shot me this look and told me to leave. Is it always like that for new mercs?"

Unlike the other soldiers, Frost showed at least a faint sign of empathy. "Not usually, no, but I wouldn't say it has anything to do with you being a merc." Frost paused and mulled over his next words. He could see Noah had becoming more reserved, more tense. He clearly lacked the hardened heart that most soldiers carried. "Look, Noah, there's a lot that goes into being an Engvall solider that people on the outside simply don't understand."

"Like what?"

"Well, the biggest thing for soldiers to get their heads around is that people die. A lot. Especially when going into ruins filled with ether infested creatures. Obviously, Humans aren't like Angels, and so once we're dead, we're not coming back. So to counter that pain, most soldiers don't like getting close to people. Sure, when you're stuck working with the same group year-round and your life can depend on the execution of their role, bonds will inevitably grow, but the last thing they want is to get attached to a kid they probably assume will die within minutes. It's nothing personal—it's just how people here cope knowing that any day could be their last."

Noah frowned, pulling his knees tighter into his body. He looked up to the pink sky and said, "I guess closing yourself off is how some people handle this sort of stuff, but that sounds like an awful way to live. Of course it's sad losing people close to you…but avoiding it makes the days you *are* alive pretty meaningless, no?"

Frost seemed taken by surprise. "I get the sentiments, Noah—believe me, I really do. But let me give you a word of advice. Where we're going with all these people on this ship right now…at *minimum* one of them won't make it back alive. That's the reality of our mission. So stay on guard and try to make sure that person isn't you. You'll thank me for it later."

Frost reached up and clamped onto a metal hold bar on the boat's inner wall, rising to his feet. "Now if you'll excuse me, I'm gonna go keel over in my bed for the night. Hopefully I can sleep until we hit shore." Frost gave a weak salute and started gingerly walking down the deck, leaving Noah to listen to the sounds of the sea in silence.

CHAPTER 6
A RUDE AWAKENING

The shores of Angel Island were lined with Engvall soldiers. The winds were stronger than back in Ekholm Territory, and the skies were covered in clouds.

Because there were no ports like back in Engvall, all the soldiers—including Noah—were forced to take smaller rowboats to shore.

When they arrived, there was no sign of civilization. In one sense that could be expected, since Angel Island was the complete opposite of a metropolis like Engvall.

That said, even with no civilization around, there were still signs of some Human presence.

Just offshore were thick, defined paths with small markings and ether lights jammed into the dirt. It was obvious that a fair bit of groundwork had been laid by soldiers long before Noah's arrival. At least that would make his travels to the ruins easier.

Getting the excavation equipment onto the shores took a little more effort. Engvall's boats were equipped with tows that allowed them to drag the equipment strapped to another large raft, though it was encased in wrapping to seal out the water.

Once they were set to begin travel, Bower stood at the front of all the battalions. Even though he was leader of 227, he appeared to be the most seasoned of all the battalion leaders, and therefore he held more command.

He began barking out orders. "All right, lot—listen up! For those new to these trails, this jungle is thick. Our paths are lined by the ether torches, so make sure you stick to the path until we get to base." He then added with a shrug, "Or take your chances in the jungle and see what happens, but just remember we're heading into high concentrations of ether. Those who have been deployed here before can tell you just what that means."

While Bower made his orders clear, Noah did his best to pay extra attention. He stood at the far end of the lineup in the back, and still nobody was willing to acknowledge his existence. Frost's words remained etched in his mind, and he tried to call upon them for comfort, but it didn't help him feel like any less of an outcast.

As much as Noah didn't enjoy being treated like he was invisible, he knew that wasn't the biggest issue his scenario presented. He could deal with being ignored. He didn't like it, but it wouldn't cost him his life. On the other hand, being treated as invisible as he traveled into an increasingly dangerous situation could be an issue. It would be nice to know that he could trust those around him to have his back. As things stood right now, it seemed fair to say that nobody would be coming to his aid if caught in a pinch.

Bower finished his speech—or, more accurately, his warning—by saying, "All right, soldiers, move out." In unison, the group marched in tight rows of five, except for Bower who led the pack at the front.

The forest was filled with all sorts of different creatures, some small enough to fit in the palm of Noah's hand, others much bigger and far more imposing. Luckily, none of them appeared to be hostile, and they hadn't yet been contaminated by high concentrations of ether. Even the soldiers were ignoring them, which indicated that they were no threat.

Other than the calls of wildlife, which were mostly drowned out by the heavy clanking of the soldier's armour, there wasn't much for Noah to admire on his path.

It was a scenic jungle walk, which under any other circumstances would've thrilled Noah. He wanted to remain focused, though. He needed to be ready for anything.

Noah walked beside Frost, looking far better now that he was on land again. Unlike the other soldiers, he wore far less armour, which probably allowed him to be more agile in battle. He wasn't saying anything along their trip, but the fact that he was willing to walk alongside Noah was a gesture that the apparent young outcast appreciated.

Along the way, Noah glanced around and noticed something rather interesting. He looked to Frost and asked, "We've seen all these creatures on our way, but none of them are stepping foot on our path. Why is that?"

Frost kept walking without turning his head, almost as if he didn't want to be ostracized for speaking to Noah, but he did toss Noah a bone by responding. "It's thanks to all the ether torches we've planted along the route. Though it's hard for Humans to detect it, most creatures with a stronger sense of smell find the aroma of ether nauseating. It's a great deterrent to keep creatures out of towns, as well as off of pathways like this."

"Oh, I see. Interesting."

After an hour of walking in the punishing sun, the squadron finally came up upon a clearing. They were much higher in the jungle now, and Noah could hear rushing water below them. But all this paled in comparison to what he could see on the horizon.

He stood at the south end of a massive stone bridge, with pillars all along the sides bearing intricate carvings. They looked somewhat like Angels, though it was hard to tell due to the decay from time. On the other side of the bridge was the entrance to the ruins. There were stone doors that had been blasted open by what one could only assume was some sort of ether cannon, because the entrance looked as though there'd been an explosion in a wall compared to the elegance of the rest of the ruins.

At a glance, it was obvious that this place was once the home of royalty. Somewhere in the pages of history, Angels of the highest order used to live here. But not now. In fact, now it was nothing but an ancient structure praying to the Guardian Angel that it wouldn't collapse.

On the opposite side of the ruins was a base camp where machines were stationed, tents pitched, and maintenance bays set up for their various equipment. Even this base camp resembled a mini city, and most certainly hadn't been set up overnight.

Bower waved a handful of soldiers to his side and started handing out orders.

Around the edges of the camp were steel sheds filled to the brim with silver canisters. One of the soldiers walked with a clipboard, making notes as he examined the canisters, each one full of ether. The sheer volume was staggering. Noah couldn't believe that the amount of ether they currently had wasn't enough to sustain them. If that didn't do the job, what would?

Other soldiers began setting up their machines, wasting no time in getting to work. Noah knew he needed to do the same, which for him was focusing on getting his mind right. But he wanted to take a moment to appreciate the sights in front of him. He thought of his grandpa, knowing how much he would've loved seeing this place.

At the front of the crew, Bower talked to a few of the already stationed soldiers, gesturing to the ether and then to the path they'd come from. He had a confident smirk as he waved them away. He turned back to his main group and ordered from the top of his lungs, "Noah! Get your ass over here!"

Noah jumped, and Bower's barked command turned all eyes toward him. He sheepishly grinned and rubbed the back of his neck before heading over to his leader.

When he reached the front, Bower slapped him on the shoulder and said, "You ready for this, kid? We're about to walk into the real deal. This ain't gonna be like fighting some rats. These things will rip you limb from limb."

Is he trying to scare me? If this was a pep talk, the battalion leader needed some work. It took a lot more than that to spook Noah.

Regardless, Noah reached around his back and drew his blade. The glaring eyes and the poor treatment he could put behind him. For now, he needed to focus on doing his job. "You bet I am," he nodded.

"Good, 'cause you're with me, and I ain't slowing down for some half-rate merc." Bower let out a hearty laugh, then walked over to a nearby table and grabbed two helmets. "Here, put this on. You're not gonna last long without it."

The strange-looking piece of equipment had two tubes on each side that came around and plugged into the round, flat snout. There were straps on the side to tighten or loosen as well, but it looked about Noah's size.

"What's this?" he asked.

"That's an ether filter helmet. Keeps the ether out of your lungs. Break that thing and you'll be dead within minutes."

Next, Bower tossed Noah a circular light with a clip on the back. This device Noah was more familiar with—it was a portable ether light. He clipped it to the chest of his jacket, tapped the front, and it turned on with a beaming yellowish light.

"Cool, this should help a lot," Noah said.

Bower pulled his own mask over his large head and strapped it on. Without another word, he started marching his way across the bridge, his Angel Crimson staying close behind. The Angel was a quiet one, only speaking when spoken to. But the power emanating off his golden axe as he followed his partner couldn't be ignored.

Noah noticed something interesting as Bower and Crimson walked side by side. The weapon that Bower had when they were back at port was now on Crimson's back. Also, Bower didn't have a weapon on him. He was a massive Human Being and his muscles could intimidate many, but if they were heading into the high level of danger area that Noah had been warned of, there was no way he could fight them barehanded.

He chose not to bring up the question, instead hoping to watch. If he thought Bower was in any danger or simply forgot, then saying something would make sense, but Bower didn't strike him as the type to overlook such a key detail.

Noah popped his mask on, fidgeting with the straps to try and make it comfortable, but there was no luck. The seal around his neck was tight and itchy, but at least no ether would be getting into his lungs, that much he was sure of. He'd just have to put up with the tightness for the time being.

Seeing Bower already halfway across the bridge, Noah rushed to catch up.

The thin ray of light emitting from his ether light shone though the opening corridor. The second Noah took his first steps inside the ruins, he felt his lungs begin to burn. His chest grew tense. "It's so hard to breath in here," he said.

"It's the high levels of ether. Your body isn't quite accustomed to it yet. Just keep that mask on and you'll be fine," Bower said quietly. His head was swiveling in all direction, his senses on high alert. That was a clear indicator to Noah that they were now in a place where threats were all around them.

Still, it was hard not to notice the intense sensations in

his body. His muscles were becoming prickly as though his limbs were going numb, and each step was far heavier than the last, like the gravity had increased.

Noah kept his eyes peeled, monitoring every part of the ruins that he could place eyes on, and observed a number of strange things. There were pictures on the walls — though in their current condition there was no making out what they were intended to look like — as well as broken statues and a balcony high above that enclosed the room. At first, Noah thought that he'd entered a throne room, or at least the remains of one.

Noah stopped when he reached the middle of the room. He could hear soldiers arriving behind him, and Bower was checking the walls for something — but he didn't know what. He glanced up at the decaying artifacts of the room, spotting seven statues that hung off the walls around the apparent throne. Some were still standing but mostly destroyed, while others were completely toppled.

But before he could pull himself away from any sightseeing, he heard a voice. *"Please find her. Find her before the others do."* The voice was faint, almost a whisper. Noah darted his eyes around and then focused on Bower who was now preoccupied with the battalion. Did he not hear the voice? Was Noah simply hearing things? He shook it off, blaming the effects of the ether. After all, it was known to cause strange hallucinations in people. Perhaps hearing voice was one of the pitfalls.

More soldiers joined them, and as a group they moved further into the ruins. As they did, Noah began to see strange particles floating in the air. They were like thousands of yellow fireflies, dancing around him. There were also jagged crystal-like structures growing in the room like weeds. Some were growing out of the floor, while others formed in the walls and on the ceiling. They were also of faint colour mixed in with their translucent crystal form, and were glowing just like an ether orb. A few of the crystal chunks had already been broken off like decaying leaves, and Noah took this to mean that they were harvested parts from a previous mission.

Bower came to a stop and said, "On your toes, team. Skitters could be anywhere."

Noah gripped his sword a little tighter, trying to ignore the heaviness in his arms. He, along with all of the other soldiers began scanning the room, sending beams of light in all different directions. It was difficult to see, even with the lights shining.

As they checked for any danger, Crimson went off ahead.

While still keeping the double-bladed axe on his back, Noah noticed something precarious.

"Hey, Bower, is it safe for Crimson to go it alone?" he asked. "It's already hard enough to see in here, and he could get ambushed."

"Nah, don't worry 'bout him. He can handle his own. Besides, his blessing is night vision, and he can see just fine down here."

Noah wanted to ask what Bower meant by "blessing," but he wouldn't be granted the time.

"Incoming! Skitters on the left!" one soldier shouted.

Bower whistled for Crimson to return, while everyone else focused their attention to the back-left corner of the room.

Hiding along the walls were about ten strange creatures. They resembled some of the same insects Noah had noticed on his trip here, with thick scaly hides and sharp pincer claws, but these were far bigger in size. Their eyes glowed green, which indicated some sort of mutation from living in the ether for so long. These "skitters," as the soldiers called them, let out a unified roar and started skittering down the walls like a stampede ready to strike. Seemed as though the name "skitters" was a fitting one.

Guns opened fire from the soldiers in the back, and beams of blue and green soared at the targets, lighting up the ruins with bright flashes. A handful of the creatures took the blasts in stride, using their outer armor as protection, but some were hit in their thin joints, losing grip on the wall and then crashing down. The ones that made it through the first wave of attacks made a mad dash for the front group, who had weapons drawn and braced for a fight.

"Let's see those skills, kid! Shape up!" Bower ordered. He jumped in front of Noah and stuck his meaty hand out, grasping at thin air. But then, through the far tunnel hurrying back, came Crimson. He whipped the axe over to Bower just in time for the man to block the incoming slash of a nearby skitter.

That's amazing! He's so strong even while dealing with the added effects of the ether, and his reflexes are incredible. How can he even see in this darkness? That's when Noah noticed a different beam of light coming from Bower's body. It was thin like his ether light, but far more concentrated. It also led directly to Crimson, his Angel, who had his hands stuck out like he was casting a spell. *Wait, are they sharing Crimson's powers? Is that what it's like to use an Angel in battle?*

Bower held off the skitter's claw, thrusting his axe in the air before toppling the skitter onto its back.

As though they were of one mind, Bower tossed the axe back into the air, where Crimson caught it in stride before slamming down on the skitter's soft underbelly. "Quit gawking and get fighting kid!" Bower yelled.

Noah snapped out of his curiosity and prepared to defend himself. Though he wished he could've used Crimson's night vision blessing, he was faintly able to see the skitters thanks to their glowing eyes.

One creature got within inches of Noah's mask, pointing its sharp talon claw in his face. It was like they knew that breaking his mask would make for an easy kill.

But thanks to watching Bower and Crimson fight, he knew exactly where the monster's weakness was. He thrust his sword upward, pushing the skitter off balance and then spotting his target. He took a wide, arching swing and managed to slash the underbelly of the skitter, forcing it to recoil with a shriek of pain.

Noah moved with a speed and grace that took the entire squadron by surprise. Even Bower froze momentarily to watch as the young merc diced his enemy with ease.

Noah came to a skidding halt, letting the two other skitters around him crumple in pieces as they hit the rocky floor.

"Don't get cocky, kid! We're not out of this yet!" Bower yelled, although there was camaraderie in his voice.

Noah braced for round two before hearing the same mysterious voice from before. *"Follow the path forward. You have the key."* Once again, nobody acted as if they heard anything, confusing Noah further.

"Hey, kid—look out!" He heard a voice shout. Noah

spun around, throwing his sword up to protect himself, but to his surprise a large icicle dropped from the sky, impaling the creature and forcing him to a dead stop.

"You need to focus or you're gonna die!" Frost yelled. He was standing in a group with other soldiers flanking him, and in his hand was one of the many ice orbs he carried.

"Right—thanks." Noah said. He shook off the mysterious voice and prepared to continue his fight.

The group held their own, finishing off the last of the ether-infested creatures before being given a moment of reprieve.

There were a number of other paths within the ruins, all likely filled with ether and ether-contaminated beings, but for the time being Bower held everyone at bay. He wanted to bring the machines in to excavate the remaining ether crystals before moving on.

As everyone was catching their breath or setting up their various machines, Noah started walking around different parts of the room. He was nearing another hallway behind the remains of the throne, although seeing inside it was impossible. Even his ether light was swallowed up by the darkness.

"*Noah, you must save her. Without her, Alterra will be no more.*"

Noah shook his head. *Who are you? And what do you mean 'Alterra will be no more'?* He stared into the void and then looked back at everyone else. Why were they not hearing this voice? What did it mean save her? And who was her? Save her from what? And the voice knew his name and that Alterra would be no more?

Noah took one final peek behind him, making sure nobody was within earshot and said, "Uh…hello, mysteri-ous voice from the void…can you give me a bit more to go on than that? Who is 'her'? And what danger?"

He felt ridiculous speaking to no one, but even more so waiting for a response.

But nothing came.

Noah had no logical reason to step forward, and yet something in his heart urged him to. The voice sounded warm, friendly even. It would be rude to just ignore it.

He closed his eyes and swallowed his trepidation be-fore putting one foot in front of the other. Deep into the darkness, he went.

Back in the central room of the ruins, machines were methodically working away. Bower surveyed his men and noticed that something was amiss. *The kid's gone? Where the hell did he go?* His eyes darted around until he spotted the obscure path behind the throne. He was sure they'd explored it before, and it was nothing more than a dead end. He stroked his chin. *I wonder if this is what the Emperor meant?*

Unaware of what was taking place in the throne room, Noah blindly followed his new path. Over time, his sur-roundings were gradually becoming brighter. Not from any true sources of light but from the density of the ether particles surrounding him. They were duplicating, which brightened up the room but also made it harder to walk, let alone breath.

Under these new conditions, one minute of walking felt like a mile. If skitters were to show up in the tunnel, he wouldn't stand a chance. And yet the further down the tun-nel he went, the more at peace the ruins around him felt.

Eventually, he arrived in a circular room. There were all sorts of intersecting lines on the floor, and in the middle sat a pedestal. A hot, burning sensation, like coal on his skin, touched his chest and he winced, grabbing at it. It was his necklace — the one Uriel had handed him right before he'd left. When he pulled it away from his neck, he noticed the intense glow radiating from it.

"What the hell are you doing, kid? I thought I told everyone to stick with the group!"

Noah spun around at the sound of Bower's voice. The battalion leader grumbled as he emerged from the shadows before realizing something. "Well, this is different… last time we came here it was just a dead end."

"What do you suppose this room is?" Noah asked. He wasn't sure if he was in trouble for wandering off or about to be praised for finding something of interest.

"I don't know…but whatever it is, I have a feeling the Emperor's gonna want to know about it." Bower knelt down, running his fingers in the grooves of the etched floor. The ether did little to impede his movements compared to Noah. When he glanced up, he placed eyes on the pedestal and said, "Is there anything we can do with that?"

Noah walked over to examine it, still clutching his necklace in his hand. He could feel the searing heat melting his skin as he got closer to their focal point.

The pedestal showed the same decay from time as the rest of the ruins, but there was still an indented outline on top, shaped by a pair of Angel wings. Noah examined the indent and then his necklace. They were a perfect match.

Bound by an invisible force, something moved his hand without permission, fitting the necklace into the stone indent.

The grooves in the floor began to bleed white, until the room's floor and walls shone with bright lines.

In the back, Bower stood in awe, watching as the room began to light up. *The Emperor was right.*

Caught up in the light show, the ground below Noah's feet started to quake. The lines were beginning to form cracks in the floor, and rocks from the ceiling started caving in. Was this Noah's doing?

"Hey, kid! Whatever the hell you're doing, you'd better stop!"

"I'm not doing anything!" Noah yelled back, the panic in his voice far more evident than in Bower's.

Bower hopped back into the tunnel's entrance. Boulders came crashing down in front of him, cutting off any vision to Noah or the room. He punched the rocks with his full might but there was no breaking through the barricade. "Damn it, kid—this wasn't part of the deal!"

Noah could no longer feel the stone floor below his feet. He tried to look down, but all he saw was darkness. He was floating in space, in a void. There were no more ether particles, no sounds…it was like his body was no longer in existence. He reached for his face and realized that there was no mask. Or *was* there? He couldn't feel his face. He couldn't feel anything. *Is this what it's like to die?* He thought.

His eyes became blurry as he tried to stumble his way forward. Despite his weak vision, he could see white lines in the distance. *"Follow the light, Noah. Begin your journey with her,"* a distant voice called out. It sounded like it was coming from the light. Noah tried to stumble forward, but something was gripping his body.

What is happening? he thought, panicking. In the distance, he could make out the doors approaching closer as the light become more prominent. They were magical in appearance, adorned with stained-glass art of a woman.

He couldn't feel his legs moving and he certainly wasn't walking of his own accord, but there was no doubt he was being taken somewhere. He could hear muffled shouts from the other side of the darkness. They sounded liked Bower but were fading into nothing once he was beyond the stained-glass doors. Finally granted light, he looked down and noticed his trinket back in his hand, this time glowing with more energy than ever before. The burning sensation had stopped, and he gradually felt his feet under him again.

What…just happened? Noah looked around his new surroundings. This room was much more intimate and rather plain, but also more futuristic looking. It was like a giant empty laboratory.

There was nowhere for him to go, but he realized that his body was feeling normal. He could breathe naturally and there were no ether particles in the air. He slipped off his mask momentarily and took a few quick breaths to make sure. With that established, he fixed his attention on the only other oddity in the room.

It came from the back wall, which looked far more futuristic than the rest of the room. Attached to the wall was a metal coffin with all sorts of ancient markings on it.

Noah approached it with curiosity. The top was made of glass and caked in layers of dust. He cleaned it off with his forearm and peered inside.

It's a young woman. Was it her voice I was hearing before?

He couldn't take his eyes off the sleeping beauty. Her arms folded on her chest, her platinum blonde hair resting down her back. She looked at peace in her long slumber.

Noah didn't want to wake the resting woman, but when he looked around his entirely white confines, he saw nowhere to go. There wasn't a door he could just walk out of.

Seeing no other option, he decided to pry on the glass.

The latches refused to budge.

Smashing the glass wasn't an option either — he didn't want to hurt the woman inside. His eyes drifted to the top of the coffin, and he spotted a beveled indent like the one he saw marked on the pedestal. He gasped, tapping his chest and realizing that his necklace was back around his neck, but the radiating heat was gone.

I wonder? He unstrapped the piece of jewellery and, treating it like a key, took the bottom of his necklace and inserted it into the slot. When he did, the lights on the coffin turned white, blinking repeatedly.

Then the necklace suddenly disintegrated in Noah's hand. It first turned into white particles before fading away, until there was no sign of its existence.

"Uh…was that *supposed* to happen?" he wondered aloud.

The hatches on the coffin unlocked, and once again he was overtaken by a blinding ray of light. He closed his eyes, but when he opened them he still remained in the white void.

More confused than before, he peeked into the metal casket once again and gasped, "She's gone! But where'd she go?" He whipped his head left and right, frantically searching.

But nothing.

Then he heard the sound of a woman adjusting her throat. "Ahem…looking for me?"

The voice startled Noah, who spun around and hopped backwards reactively. But in his haste, he smacked into the coffin, tumbling over backwards and landing on his head.

His eyes fluttered open again, now staring at a pair of white and gold shoes with a small diamond on the front. He heard a breathless giggle before glancing up a little further.

Standing in front of him was a tall young woman, her platinum hair long and with powerful sapphire eyes. But those weren't what caught Noah's attention. It was her regal appearance—the elegance in her walk, the way she exuded power. Her presence was intimidating in many ways.

She was covered in strange, white and gold armour that fit her body perfectly. It also made her look like a powerful warrior, one of royal decent.

Noah opened his mouth, but nothing came out. He instead pointed to the coffin, then back to the woman.

The newly awakened woman raised an eyebrow. "You might want to get up."

Her voice was just as powerful as her attractiveness, with some aggression added in for good measure. She sounded like a woman who knew what she wanted.

Noah got to his knees, squeezed his eyes shut, and started gently slapping his cheeks. "I've had some strange dreams but this…this takes the cake."

"What're you doing?" the woman asked.

"I'm trying to wake myself up."

She loomed over Noah, hands on her hips. "You *are* awake. I'm the one who's been asleep for the last 300 years."

Noah glanced up, got to his feet, and focused his attention on her. "So…I'm awake?"

"Yep."

"This isn't a dream?"

"Nope."

"So Angel Island…the Engvall army and Bower…all that's real?"

"Well, I don't know about any of that, but you're definitely awake."

Noah took a few deep breaths, touching every inch of his body. The tenderness of his bruises, the small scrapes on his arms—all those sensations couldn't be replicated in a dream.

"I really *am* awake…" he whispered. He looked back and stared at the woman. "Okay, if I really am awake, then boy do I have a lot of questions."

"Lucia."

"Huh? Lucia?"

"Yes, that's my name. And you're Noah, right?"

"Uh, yeah, but how'd you know that? Have we met before?"

"Not exactly. To be honest, I don't really know how I knew it. I just sort of did. I guess it comes with unity."

"Unity…you mean like when an Angel and Human are linked?" Noah was confused, but when he stared into Lucia's sapphire eyes, he could see the powerful glow synonymous with all Angels. He gasped, "Wait…but that means…"

She nodded and snapped her fingers. In a split second, they were back in the intimate, futuristic room where Noah had first found the coffin.

"Whoa…how did you…?"

"I'm not really sure why that happens when unity is created — it just sort of does. It's like our subconscious minds meeting or something," Lucia shrugged.

Finally, Noah noticed something that signified his bond and put to rest any thoughts that he might be imagining all this. He felt a small ring of gold and blue meld onto his finger. When he looked at Lucia's finger, she wore a matching ring.

Curious, he tried to remove the ring to examine it, but with no luck.

"What are you doing?" Lucia asked.

"I was just seeing if I could take the ring off."

Lucia rubbed her eyes and said, "These rings are a symbol of our unity; it's what bonds us together. So no, you can't just take it off. However, that actually brings up a rather interesting question." Her face grew cross. "How did some random child get his hands on my soul stone to wake me up?" She dominantly put her hands on her hips again and leaned in close to Noah.

Noah stepped back hitting the coffin, but this time he managed to stay upright. "Uh…well you see…" he chuckled nervously, "I don't really know. It was a gift. I had no idea it was a soul stone. I've never used a soul stone in my life."

Lucia's anger faded and she observed Noah's boyish innocence. If he was lying to her, he had one incredible poker face. But he didn't strike her as a bold-faced liar. He didn't seem the type.

"Okay…and this person who gave it to you…any clue how they would've got his hands on such an artifact? It was supposed to have been locked away."

Noah frowned, shaking his head. "Locked away? No, I don't know how he got it. Honestly, I didn't even know he had it until yesterday."

"Hmm…" Lucia eyed him with scrutiny and then started to fidget with her own ring. "Fine, but if I find out you're lying to me, you're as good as dead."

Noah laughed meekly at the threat and smiled. "Okay, it's a deal." He took a seat on the edge of the coffin and said, "But now you've got to answer a question for me. And you're not allowed to lie either."

"All right, I guess that's fair. Shoot."

"Where are we? And why were you locked away down here?"

"First off, that's two questions. But honestly, I don't think I can answer either of them." Lucia's cool demeanor softened as she took a seat next to Noah. "Ever since I woke up, I've been trying to remember things…the past, my former life, how I ended up here…but I can't. It's like everything in my mind is covered by a fog. I know it's there—I can feel it. Like there are memories that I should remember…but I just can't think of them. The only thing that came to my mind just then was your name, and the memory of my soul stone being placed in here. Also, there's another person, but I can't recall a face…it's like I'm staring at a shadow when I think of them."

"That must be tough. I can't imagine what it would be like to lose all my memories. That would be really sad. Not remembering your family, your friends, and all the great things you probably did as an Angel."

Noah hopped up and turned to face Lucia, grinning. "You said we're now unified, right? You're my Angel?"

"I mean, I guess technically, though I'm not really sure that's how this is supposed to work."

"Well, then—let's go see if we can find anybody who might know why you were locked away in here and see if they have any clue about how to get your memories back. Come on, it'll be like a big adventure. I'll bet you used to go on adventures all the time."

Lucia felt a rare warmth in her heart. She smiled weakly and said, "Really?"

"Of course! You're my Angel now after all—we're supposed to be like a team, and I know that if I didn't have my memories that would be really tough, so we should see if we can find anyone who knows about you. Angels can live for hundreds of years, right? That means there must be someone who knows about your past."

"Thank you, Noah, that really means a lot to me," Lucia said, standing. "But before we do anything, since you didn't exactly resonate with my soul stone, we should probably check just to be sure." She held her left hand out, and a string of light flowed into Noah's chest.

Suddenly he felt this warmth fill him from head to toe. His nose twitched with a strange tingle, and he could feel that his senses were on high alert.

"*Well, it seems pretty cut and dry to me. We're unified,*" Lucia said. Only her mouth didn't move.

Noah carefully stared at his new Angel, and so she spoke again, her mouth still shut. "*When we're unified, it's like we're of one mind. My thoughts are your thoughts; my power is your power. That's why you can hear me.*"

Curious, Noah tried it as well, thinking, "*I can't believe it—I'm partners with a real Angel. This is so cool!*"

Lucia snapped her fingers, breaking the string of light and said, "You don't have a lot of experience with Angels, do you?"

Noah shook his head. "Not really. The only Angels I've ever seen are the ones in the Engvall army, but they never really speak."

Suddenly a thought dawned on him. "Crap, I totally forgot about Bower and the others. They probably think I'm long dead by now." He started glancing around hoping to spot an exit, but they were all caved in. "Well, this might be a problem, as we don't really have another way out of here. So unless the other army guys come looking for me, I don't see how we're going to escape."

"I don't think that'll be necessary." Lucia smirked and lifted her hand to the side, and out of thin air materialized a magnificent sword. It was monstrous, with gold trim and a white blade. In the middle of the blade was the same symbol on Noah's necklace. And despite its size, she wielded it as she would a butter knife.

"Whoa, where've you been hiding that thing this whole time?"

"Let's just call it divine intervention. Now there's plenty of ether around here and I can use that to boost my strength." She winked and waved Noah away from the landslide of rocks. "Oh, but before I do that, do you have anything to protect yourself from the ether? This room is pretty safe, but I can sense that the other side of this wall has enough ether in the air to kill a mortal."

"Oh, right." Noah grabbed his mask off his belt and put it back on, flashing a thumbs up.

Lucia held the tip of her sword out until it scraped along

the rocks. "Now watch and learn. You're about to witness the power of an Angel!" With blinding precision, she carved out a star made from the trailing light of her sword's movements before finishing it off with a ferocious thrust. Her hair blew back as her body gave off a radiant glow.

Enchanted by these moves, Noah stared at Lucia, barely noticing the rocks shattering into dust.

"Wow, you're really good. I could barely keep up with your movements."

Lucia shrugged. "I'm still a bit rusty, but it'll come back over time, I'm sure. Now come on. I want to see some daylight. It's been a *long* time."

With Lucia doing much of the heavy lifting, she and Noah were able to follow the path back, disposing of any creatures that dared to approach them. Noah was never one to be cocky, even though he knew he was skilled. But when watching Lucia, he felt like an amateur. The grace in which she moved and the way she anticipated her opponent's attacks was brilliant. It was like she could see what was about to happen before it did.

He couldn't help but wonder if he'd be granted such strength in the same way Bower and Crimson were able to share their power. But he'd worry about that later. For now, he didn't want to keep Bower and the others searching and fearing the worst for him.

They reached what remained of the main throne room, and to Noah's surprise, it was empty. Most of the crystals had been extracted, and even the corpses of the ether-infested creatures had decayed into piles of waste.

"Where is everyone?" Noah whispered. The hollow silence left an eerie feeling in the air.

"You think they left? I mean they probably thought you were dead," Lucia said a little too flippantly.

Noah remained silent and began making his way to the ruins' exit. The closer he got, the more he could hear the powerful rumblings of machinery on the outside. He picked up his pace, Lucia remaining close behind.

When they finally reached the entrance, the air became fresher and small beams of light poured in through the jagged cracks.

Noah stopped and smiled at Lucia. "You ready to see the world again?"

"Yeah, I'm kind of excited, actually. Three hundred years isn't exactly a brief vacation."

"Well then, let's get going! Everyone is going to be so shocked to see you."

The two stepped forward, enveloped by the light. Lucia took a deep breath of the clear air, sighing with content. She glanced around her surroundings, seeing the outer walls of the ancient ruins. Then she noticed the pillars with Angel-like symbols on them. Everything felt different yet all at once the same.

"Hey, there's Bower and the others," Noah said, gesturing to the opposite side of the stone bridge where the army's camp was set up. The new union started walking across the bridge, but then Lucia grabbed Noah's arm and came to a stop.

"What's wrong?" Noah asked.

Lucia was picking up on some tension in the air, which Noah was oblivious to.

It was true that soldiers were lined up at the other end of the bridge, but what Noah failed to notice was that they all had their guns locked and loaded. Behind them were the large-scale, machine-like robots from before, except this time the canisters on the sides were filled to the brim with sloshing, blue liquid. Pure ether. It appeared that they were preparing for something drastic.

"Don't you think this is a little weird?" Lucia asked. "Are you sure these people are your friends?"

Noah maintained his optimistic grin and said, "Yeah, of course—we're all on the same team here."

On the opposite side of the bridge, Bower had his back turned to Noah, giving orders to the soldiers. Crimson stood at his side, and neither noticed Noah and his new Angel.

Noah began crossing the bridge and waving his arms as he called out, "Hey Bower!" The squad leader's ears perked up. The familiar voice forced him to turn around, his eyes cross as he spotted Noah. He was visibly confused.

"Kid...how did you—?"

"We made it out of that rockslide. And wait until you see who I met!" But then Noah came to a stop when he heard Bower's angry grunt.

Narrowing his focus, Bower then looked past Noah and spotted Lucia, her eyes glowing brightly. Angel eyes. "So she *does* exist...the Angel of Death," Bower uttered in contempt. His face became sad, and his shoulders slouched. "You just couldn't go away peacefully, could you, kid?" A thin string of light formed from Bower to Crimson, and in a blink he dashed forward, his axe ready to pierce flesh.

Stunned by this reaction, Noah never even reached for his sword. Luckily, Lucia was more prepared. She flew forward and crossed swords with Bower, shielding Noah from certain death.

"You've got some nerve attacking an unsuspecting boy like that! What's your deal?" Lucia barked.

"Your power precedes you, Arch Angel…or should I call you The Angel of Death?"

Lucia's body twitched at the name, her concentration faltering briefly. Bower shoved her back, putting some distance between them.

"Bower, what do you think you're doing?" Noah shouted.

"It's nothing personal, kid—this is just business. Men, capture the Arch Angel and dispose of the boy. He's of no use to us anymore." The soldiers braced their weapons, locked their aim and prepared to fire.

"But…but I don't get it! What do you mean 'it's just business'?" Noah fretted. He began to grab his sword, though he wasn't interested in fighting.

Bower held his hand to his side, indicating for his troops to hold fire. "Fine, kid. I guess every man deserves to know the reason for his death. Now listen good, 'cause I'm not repeating myself. That Angel behind you is something quite special to this world. And for that reason, the Emperor wants her. Admittedly, I didn't really believe him when he told me she existed, but it turns out the greedy bastard was right. He was confident she lay in these ruins, but we could never find her. We needed two things. A key, and a heart deemed worthy by the Guardian Angel. I still can't believe you had both…and yet here we are. I'm not sure how the Emperor knew you carried the key with you, especially after he spent years searching for it, but now that the Arch Angel has risen, she's coming with us."

Noah tried to understand this information, but he didn't have time—there were more pressing issues. He reached back and drew his blade with conviction, saying, "Uriel was right—I should've never trusted the Emperor. Well, too bad. You can tell the Emperor he's *not* getting Lucia. I won't let you lay a hand on her."

"Noah...thank you." Lucia held her hands to her heart.

"Sorry, kid—wrong answer." Bower raised his hand to the sky, shouting "Men, open fire!"

A violent wave of rainbow beams shot out like fireworks in the night. Noah braced to go on the defensive, doing what he could to deflect the blasts, but even he knew that there was no chance to defend himself from them all. But that didn't matter. Lucia was his friend, and he refused to let her fall into the hands of a crooked man like Emperor Engvall.

"Noah!" Lucia cried out. Like a reflex, she thrust her hands forward and a massive opaque wall of light formed in front of them. The blasts were absorbed by the shield, like rain hitting the ocean. The army kept firing rounds with the heavy machines joining in, but nothing could penetrate her barrier.

The sounds of ether bullets hitting the shield jostled Noah to open his eyes. It sounded like they were underwater as the shield rippled with each hit. He glanced to his left, seeing Lucia with her arms outstretched, casting fluttering beams of light into the wall.

"Noah, you need to run! I can't hold this forever!" Lucia said through gritted teeth. The pain in her eyes, the twitching in her arms as each blast pelted her barrier—it was all proof of her claim. But Noah shook his head. "No, I'm not leaving you! You're my Angel, and that means it's my job to protect you as much as it's your job to protect me. We're a team, remember!"

Noah could see cracks starting to form in Lucia's barrier, which was weakening with each massive blast. Simple gunfire was easy enough to handle, but the large ether cannons were doing significant damage.

Finally, a single blast broke through their wall and streaked toward Lucia's chest.

Noah dashed in front, throwing his sword up to block the bullet.

Clank.

The beam cracked his blade on impact, but held on just long enough to deflect the second bullet that also broke through.

"Please, Noah! It's me they want—not you!"

"No! I'm not leaving!" Noah shouted vehemently. "I said I would help you find your memories again, and that's what I'm gonna do!"

Trying to think of a solution, Noah shielded off the third and final blast that squeaked through. But as it clashed with his blade, the top of his sword shattered, soaring through the air. "Grandpa's sword!" he cried.

Without a weapon and Lucia breaking down, Noah had to look for an escape plan.

Furiously examining his options, Noah picked up on the swaying sounds of the river below him. It wasn't much, but it might be a sign of hope. The question was—how could he pull it off? He lacked a weapon strong enough to break the bridge, and the walls were far too tall to climb without making himself an easy target.

Lucia could slice the bridge with ease, he was confident in that, but she couldn't drop her shield without the two of them becoming filled with holes. They'd need something else to shield them.

He turned back to the onslaught of bolts continuing to hail down on them. Through the chaos, he spotted one lone soldier — he had his gun strapped to his back, refusing to shoot. Through his half-shielded helmet he noticed the red beard, and around his waist a series of ice-blue orbs. Frost, the only man who'd talk to him back on the boat, appeared to be ignoring orders.

Then Noah was struck with an idea. He reached for his belt, plucking off the ice orb that Frost had gifted him. He gripped the sphere in his left hand, feeling the cool ether chill his blood. He took a step back next to Lucia and said, "I have an idea."

"I'm all ears at this point, but make it quick!" Her legs were beginning to give out as she channeled a little more power into her barrier.

"Do you think you can break this bridge?" Noah asked.

For a split-second, Lucia lost concentration as she turned to fix her shock on Noah. But realizing that she needed to maintain composure, she held strong and said, "I mean, yes, but I'm a little busy at the moment! So unless you can deflect all those incoming blasts, we'll be dead before I can even blink!"

"Just trust me, okay?!" Noah smiled reassuringly, which perplexed Lucia given their circumstances. Still, there was something about the innocence of his face. It carried a confidence that reassured her.

"Well, I guess I don't have much of a choice now, do I?"

"Nope!" Noah took a few strides forward and then raised his free hand out in front of him. He concentrated all his strength into his ice orb, and the chill in the air grew freezing cold.

"Wall of ice!" he yelled, thrusting the orb high into the air. The orb began to glow pale blue, and a swirl of snow-white wind surrounded Noah before he cast his hand downward. Rising from the base of the bridge, just on the inside of the barrier was a new wall — one made entirely of ice like a giant glacier. He turned to Lucia and ordered, "Now! Destroy the bridge!"

The two could hear blasts repeatedly clanking away as the bridge shook below their feet. Noah could also hear Bower shouting, but it was too muffled to understand.

The ice would never hold out as long as Lucia's barrier had, but it would be long enough to serve its purpose.

Lucia ceased her barrier and summoned her sword. She jammed it into the bedrock of the bridge, and cracks started to form. Rays of light rose up from the jagged openings and, piece by piece, it began crumbling.

"Hold on tight!" Noah yelled as he ran back toward Lucia. He grabbed her around the waist just in time as half the bridge crashed in on itself.

The two shrieked as they became weightless, plummeting at high speed into the rushing river below. With a vicious cannon ball splash, they were washed downstream — their next destination unknown.

CHAPTER 7
THE ANGEL OF DEATH?

Insects chirped in the night as Noah rolled onto his back.

"Ugh…what happened?"

His eyes fluttered open and he stared up at the twinkling stars and the pale moonlight. The waves of the sea running through Angel Island and the Kerfoot region were surprisingly calming and close to putting Noah back to sleep, but he fought the urge. Lifting his arms above his head, he felt the tender bruises in his body. They made him wince and felt like added weight to his body. Now he wasn't even sure if he could get to his feet.

Attempting to force himself up, he realized that the left side of his body was pinned. He twisted his head and quickly realized why. A blonde-haired girl rested firmly on his arm—her eyes were closed, her body soaking wet, and she was shivering. Noah's eyes widened and suddenly it all came flooding back to him: checking the ruins, meeting Lucia, being betrayed and then attacked by Bower and the Engvall army…and, of course, smashing the bridge before plummeting hundreds of feet below into the gushing water. Noah assumed they must've washed up on shore, dazed and disoriented. After all, that's certainly how he felt.

His ears perked up and tried to pin down a specific noise, but there was nothing except the softness of insect chirps. That meant no ether bullets and no marching of soldiers. They were safe, at least for the time being. He sighed a breath of relief and decided on his next course of action. Warming up Lucia.

Trying hard not to disturb the Arch Angel, Noah wiggled his arm free from Lucia's waist before getting to his knees. The Angel's body shivered intensely. *This isn't much, but it should help a bit.* Noah took off his jacket and spread it out over his new companion's body. Their height difference was a bit problematic, but it was the best Noah could come up with.

I'm gonna need to make a fire to warm her up. He monitored his surroundings, scanning for available materials. Where they were wasn't all that different from the paths to the ruins. One half led to the thick forest, which had a number of different areas to explore, while behind them was the beach they'd washed up on. There wasn't much use going back that way — the water ran down stream and the giant, cliffside rocks leading up to the ruins weren't designed to be scaled.

Then he managed to spot an item that could prove useful. Much of the bridge, which he'd had a hand in toppling, had washed up on shore with them. Although a decent amount of it remained in massive chunks, unmovable by mortal or Angel, some smaller rocks that chipped off could be used to build a fire pit. Adding some branches and leaves that were no doubt available in the forest, and he was in business. Once he could make a fire pit, he needed one more thing, and luckily this one would be the easiest to find. He unclipped the orange and red ether orb, checking it for water damage. The orb appeared unharmed from its opposing element.

With the fire in place, he reached around his back and grabbed what remained of his sword. This time, there'd be no repairing it. After being shattered from the barrage of ether bullets, there was little left of its steel blade, or even the newly formed hilt created by Uriel.

Though the loss of his prized possession was tough, it had met a fitting end. It had saved lives, and he knew that his grandpa would be proud.

Noah turned back to look at Lucia, vividly recalling her own weapon. It was unlike anything he'd ever seen. Even the few Angels he'd witnessed in recent days couldn't compare. There was definitely something special about Lucia. He knew that now — especially if a man like Emperor Engvall wanted her. He smiled, happy to have met his own Angel, and one so unique.

But his smile slowly turned into a frown. *She's barely just woke up, and yet she's already being hunted by people. That must be tough to deal with. I hope she's okay.*

In wake of everything that had happened, many questions floated through Noah's mind. In particular, he wondered about the conversation with Bower. That moment above all others stuck in his brain, refusing to quiet. At first, the information had failed to register as he'd had no time to process it, but sitting there in the serenity of the forest, he was able to look back and reflect.

It was all beginning to make sense. Why nobody would talk to him and why he was repeatedly shunned on the boat. They all probably understood the assignment. He was going to play his role in bringing Lucia to the army, and then he'd be executed for his efforts. Worse off, it would've been in a place where nobody would've ever found his body, allowing them to frame it like an accident. A cunning plan that only Emperor Engvall would come up with, or at least that's what Noah imagined Uriel telling him. As was often the case, she'd turned out to be right all along.

But there was a second revelation on his mind relating to his grandpa's necklace—Lucia's soul stone. How did he find such a rare relic, and why did he keep it hidden for so long? Was it because he knew that Emperor Engvall was after it?

Noah thought back to the unity ceremony, and then a different question came to mind. From his moderate understanding of how Angels worked, they were birthed from their soul stone when they united with a Human. But Lucia was already a being when he found her. Why was that?

He thought about asking the Angel herself, but figured she wouldn't remember. If he wanted answers, he'd need to stick to his original promise of helping Lucia get her memories back.

But where would he even begin? In situations like this, usually he would ask Uriel. But he'd need to find a way home if he were to do that.

This brought up another question: was heading home even an option anymore? With Berrios being so close to Engvall, how would the Emperor handle his survival? Not well, Noah imagined. And bringing Lucia closer to the man who was after her? Not a chance. Of course, all this was moot for the time being, since getting back to his region would be another issue all together. All he could do was hope that the people of Berrios would be safe.

As the night carried on, Noah sat by the edge of the fire, holding his palms out and filling them with warmth. His hair and clothing managed to dry out rather quickly, and he moved Lucia closer to the fire. He learned that she was quite the heavy sleeper, though surprisingly light to carry. Was that due to her essence of being an Angel?

Finally able to rest, he leaned back and inhaled the aroma of the bonfire. It reminded him of his days with his grandfather. Staying out in the forests near Berrios, sleeping under the stars, sitting around camp fires, and eating whatever they managed to hunt that afternoon. Those memories brought about some semblance of joy in an otherwise never-ending day.

Noah slumped his shoulders and sighed. He missed his grandpa so much, and life just wasn't the same without his guidance.

But he could always look on the bright side. He fixed his gaze on Lucia and couldn't help but smile. He had a new friend, and an Angel at that. And if the earlier, frantic events were what it took to meet his Angel, then he was just fine with the way things had played out. He was excited to see what the future held, and to help Lucia regain her memory. It was the sort of thing his grandpa would've done.

A little later in the night, Noah heard a mild rustling beside him. Lucia yawned widely before pushing herself up to her knees and pulling the blanket around her closer to her body. But when she felt its leathery texture, she noticed it wasn't a blanket at all—it was Noah's jacket. She turned to Noah and saw him staring back at her, then focused on the fire. There were still remnants of the bridge sticking out of the water, jogging her memory.

"Did…did you do all this? she asked.

Noah grinned. "Yep. It wasn't tough—all the supplies I needed were close by. Besides, you were shaking pretty bad when we washed up on shore. I didn't want you catching a cold or something. Wait…can Angels even catch colds?"

"Not really." She laughed softly at his innocent question before rising to her feet. She stretched out her arms and handed Noah his jacket back. "Thank you, I really appreciate it. You're a good person, Noah."

Noah noted an air of sadness about her as her face glowed red in the light of the flickering flames. Worry, sorrow, fear—all of it played in those glowing sapphire eyes.

The two listened to the crackles of the fire for a few moments before Noah asked, "Is something wrong?"

Lucia faced the fire and whispered, "I'm sorry."

Surprised by this, Noah twisted his body to face Lucia more directly. "Sorry for what? You haven't done anything wrong."

"It's just…" Lucia tried to find the right words, but they wouldn't come. She may have been intimidating when they'd first met, but now was something entirely different. "Let me ask you something. Do you know how to break unity between a Human and an Angel?"

Noah gave her a puzzled look and shook his head. "No, does it have something to do with the rings on our fingers?"

"Sort of, but it's a bit more complicated than that. It's funny…I can barely remember anything about my past, and yet there's still so much information I *do* remember. For starters, they used to call unity between an Angel and a Human the most unbreakable bond in Alterra, because the only way for it to be broken is through the death of the Human. When the Human dies, their ring shatters and the Angel's spirit is said to return to the Celestial Realm, where their soul stone loses its power. At least for a time. But unlike Humans, our soul stones will eventually regain their life, and when they do we can be reborn through unity with a new mortal. It's sort of confusing, but in a way, Angels can never die. We just move from one mortal to the next over time."

"Oh." Noah paused, confused. "But I still don't think I understand what you're apologizing for."

Lucia sighed gently. "Because you and I are now unified. That means that our powers are one. Which also means that for as long as you're with me, your life will now be in danger. I don't know about this Emperor Engvall, but it seems pretty clear that he wants me as *his* Angel, and he's willing to kill you to make that happen. And now that I'm united with you, the only way for him to have my power for himself would be by killing you. That makes you target number one. Your life is in danger, and it's all because I exist. It's clear that you didn't know what you were doing when you woke me up. This isn't something you asked for, but now our lives are intertwined together."

With a shrug, Noah showed no signs of concern. "I

wouldn't worry about that too much." He smiled faintly, but that couldn't mask the sadness in the air.

"Don't you understand what I just said?" Lucia asked.

"Yeah, I understand. The Emperor needs to kill me to take you. But based on last night, he wouldn't think twice about it. And regardless, it's not like you chose to unite with me either. I was the one who caused that, so there's no reason to blame yourself. As for the army and what they tried to do to us…it's not right, even if they were just following orders. Also, in the end, you used that shield power of yours to protect my life. You saved me, and that's good enough for me to trust you. Besides, I promised to help you find your memories, and I always keep my promises." Noah stood up, brushing away any residual sadness and smiled. "It's like you said, our fates are now intertwined. Whether you like it or not, we're stuck together! So no more apologies and no more sad faces. If Engvall wants you, then they'll have to go through me first."

"I…don't know what to say. That means a lot. Thank you." Lucia smiled genuinely as Noah's warm words comforted her. "Then as your Angel, I'll do my best to protect you, as well. As long as I'm around, this Emperor Engvall won't be laying a hand on you."

"I'd say you've already done a good job of that. You stopped Bower from killing me, and you even managed to hold off all those ether bullets. But I have to ask — how did you create such a barrier? I've never seen anything like it. Even with Engvall ether tech, they couldn't do that. It was amazing."

"Oh, it wasn't much — honestly. I guess you could consider it one of my blessings."

"Blessings? Wait, I remember Bower talking about his Angel's blessing," Noah said, scratching his brow. "He said something about night vision."

Lucia giggled. "You really *don't* have much experience with Angels, do you?"

Noah shook his head. The innocence in his eyes astounded Lucia. Even after attempts made on his life, he still had a youthful enthusiasm to him.

"Okay…well, let me explain things a bit. Every Angel has blessings. They're like our powers, and it's one of the things that make Angels unique. All Angels have different blessings when they're born. Some have astounding healing capabilities, some provide speed and strength, while others have more moderate blessings like a great sense of taste. I suppose this Angel you're talking about had some form of night vision as their blessing. But one of my blessings is casting barriers of light. I don't know why it came to mind when it did, but it was just an instinct, I guess. You, on the other hand…" She grabbed Noah's hands, holding his palms. "That giant wall of ice you created on the bridge. I've seen Angels that could do that sort of magic, but never a mortal. You formed it from ether, right?"

"Yeah, but it takes a little more than just ether to pull off." Noah reached to his belt and pulled out the remains of his flame orb. "This is an ether orb. This one allows me to use fire magic, hence the red colouring. I'm not an expert on how it all works—in fact, that was sort of my first time using it, but the orb contains highly concentrated ether, and then we channel it through our body and output magic, just like the Ancestors used to."

He handed the orb to Lucia, and she cusped it in her

hands. Her fingers tingled from the warmth as she tried to wrap her head around such power. "The feeling I get holding this orb is just like the feeling I get when I use my blessing. That's quite the handywork. I didn't think mortals would be capable of such things."

"As much as I hate to say it, Emperor Engvall's family and the army are the ones who managed to create them. They've created an entire Empire by using incredible amounts of ether to create things unimaginable. That's what I was led to believe our mission was. The Emperor personally hired me to help join this mission to excavate ether to help sustain his Empire."

"Sounds like a swell guy." Lucia rolled her eyes then handed the orb back to Noah. He attached it back onto his hip pocket.

"They do have limited uses though before the ether runs dry," he told her. "And I think if you use too much, the ether can still harm mortals, so we need to be careful. This one doesn't have much left, but it was enough for me to make this fire."

For the next hour or so, the two chatted, kindly and eagerly learning from each other. It also felt liberating. They were free from the fear brought on by the Engvall army.

For Lucia, contact with the outside world was much-needed, and Noah had made a new friend. Someone he could rely on and someone he shared a special bond with. It was a great feeling, and one he hadn't experienced in a long time.

The night air was warm from the fire as soft splashes from the waves washed up on shore. After much talking, Lucia yawned before stretching her hands to the sky.

"You'd think that someone who was asleep for so long would be a little more awake," Noah laughed. He folded his jacket into a pillow and set it on the ground. "But I'm sure that using so much power the way you did after just waking up wasn't easy. You should try and get some more sleep. I'll keep watch through the night to make sure that no Engvall soldiers show up. It looks like we've floated pretty far downstream though, so I'm sure we're safe."

Lucia glanced around and said, "I suppose this is the best we're gonna do for the night." Their location certainly wasn't ideal, and the dirt wouldn't exactly provide a comfortable sleep, but based on the circumstances it was better than nothing.

Despite Lucia's attempts to hide the weariness in her body, she continued to yawn—Noah's assumptions were spot on. It was strange that she couldn't recall much, though for some reason she was sure that using her blessings had never been so tiring. It should've been little more than a drop in the bucket in terms of her power's capabilities. Maybe she was just rusty from a long slumber, but it felt like more than that, like something was stealing away her energy supply.

But those were issues to deal with later. For now, she needed to rest, and she assumed that Noah needed his rest as well.

"Are you sure you have the energy to stay up?" she asked him. "It's not like you've exactly been taking it easy, and you even built this whole fire while I've slept already."

"Don't worry, it's fine. I got plenty of sleep when we were knocked out. If anything happens, I'll wake you up and we can run, but I don't think we have much to worry about at this point."

There should've been an uneasiness for Lucia that would force her to refuse sleep. Even being unified, to trust a complete stranger with her safety was a lot, but none of that seemed to apply with Noah. There was a caring certainty in his words. When he spoke, it eased any mistrust Lucia may have had. In her heart, she believed it would all be okay. She could place her trust in him, and together they'd find a way.

Losing the battle against keeping her eyes open, she nodded and said, "Okay, but don't let me sleep too long—we're gonna need to find a way out of this place soon or those Engvall guys will be on us before we know it."

Noah agreed as she rested her head on his jacket, the warmth of the fire her blanket.

For the rest of the night, Noah gazed at the stars, his mind filling with empty thoughts until the sun finally rose over the horizon. There was no sign of the Engvall army, just as he'd predicted, and any creatures in their midst were kept away thanks to the ether in the fire.

There was a distinct difference between elements like fire, water, or ice when it came from an ether orb compared to regular ether in the air. The smell was more potent, and so was the ferocity, which Noah assumed was a by-product of the highly concentrated ether levels needed to create the orbs. That potency also ensured that no creatures would approach them, just like how the army used their ether torches to line their paths.

When Lucia rose from her slumber, she noticed Noah sitting with his back up against one of the broken slabs of the bridge, the hilt of his shattered sword in his hands. She could see the intensity with which he admired it, the longing eyes of someone fixated on something with great importance.

She got up and walked over to him, saying, "I'm sorry about your sword yesterday. It looks like it was really special to you." There was some worry in her words, as if knowing that she was broaching a sensitive topic, but Noah glanced up with those innocent eyes that never flinched.

"Yeah, it was my grandpa's sword. He used it for years, and right before he passed, he handed it down to me. It's always kept me safe in battle, like he was right there beside me." Noah sighed, twirling its remnants in his hands. "I always knew that one day it would finally break…it's been through a lot. But I guess I was just hopeful I'd be able to use it a little longer."

"And you broke it trying to protect me. Noah—I'm sorry."

Those words and their sadness finally caused him to shift his tone. Noah shook his head and stood up. "He would've been proud to see his blade go down protecting someone. That was everything he stood for. It does, of course, pose a bit of a different problem. I don't have a weapon to fight with anymore, and we can't keep relying on you to expend your powers if anything attacks. I'm sure it's still too much of a strain on you."

He made a good point. Of course Lucia held the power to fight anything in their way—in particular, monsters rustling through the jungle—but her stamina was still just returning. It was best to use her strength in a pinch, and nothing more until she returned to form.

Lucia held her hands out and asked, "Can I see the hilt?"

Noah looked at her quizzically but saw no harm in this, and so he handed over the broken keepsake.

Lucia balanced the hilt on her left hand, running the fingers of her right hand along the broken grooves. As she did, it began to glow a faint gold. She moved her fingers as though she was weaving strings of light together while Noah watched in awe.

When she finished, the sword molded into a unique design of gold red and white. Relic-like carvings lined the blade, and the hilt was fanning out with similar designs and light running through it.

Lucia smiled. "I know it's a little different than what your grandpa used, but I think it should still get the job done." She admired her work, eying the red soul stone gem in the hilt. The steel sparkled like it had just been pulled out of the forge. And there was no mistaking the enchanting aura that lay in Lucia's hands. She handed it to Noah, and he stared down at it in awe.

"No way! That's really impressive. And it kind of looks like your sword. But how did you do that?"

"Believe it or not, it wasn't hard. I took my sword and merged it with your grandpa's hilt to form this blade. I guess you could call it an Angel weapon. Most Angels and mortals do this. Now I can channel my ether into your blade, allowing you to harness my strength in battle. I'm sure it'll take a little getting used to, but I promise — it'll work wonders for you."

Noah took his new sword in hand and gave it a few preliminary swipes. "It's so light, but it feels so strong. This is perfect!"

It may have had a different appearance but the same

love, comfort, and protection that warmed him when he'd used his grandpa's blade carried over to Lucia's creation.

"Oh, that's nothing. Wait until I channel my power in it, then you'll really be in for a treat." Lucia held her hands out and, just like Noah had witnessed before with Bower and Crimson, a tethering line of light flowed into his chest. A golden aura swirled around him, extending to his sword. The angular parts of the hilt emanated with bright light, while the middle of the blade's pincer formed a magnificent, glowing beam. "You should probably take it for a quick test run before we leave. Wouldn't want you overdoing it by mistake."

"Sure, but what can I use it on?"

Lucia pointed to a slab of rock that remained from the bridge. It was nothing more than an eyesore now anyway, and Noah too was curious to understand his new powers.

Lucia increased the amount of power flowing between them, and Noah's body felt like it was undergoing a metamorphosis. A mystical, divine sense of strength flowed through his blood. His eyes felt clearer, his body lighter, and even the sword in his hands felt as light as a paperweight despite its size.

Inside the blade, a ray of yellow and white light burst forward, extending the blade further into a brilliant beam. The jagged edges spun like a rotating saw blade forming a flaming ray of light.

"*I feel incredible. Is this what unity feels like?*" Noah held his hand to his heart. "*I don't even know how to describe it.*"

"*It's a special bond for sure. Together like this, we're of one mind. Now don't be shy. It's not too complicated — just focus like usual. I'll take care of the rest.*"

Noah glanced at Lucia, and then it dawned on him. *"Right, you can hear my thoughts in unity."*

"Yeah, so you'd better be careful." They both smiled, and Noah's cheeks turned red.

"Okay," Noah decided. "Let's do this."

Noah took three, lightning-fast swings. The sword left a trace of light in its path, creating a triangular shape on the bridge's remains. The blade was smooth, able to cut through the air with ease while leaving behind light with each swing. The trailing light flickered, and after a brief flash the pieces of the bridge Noah had attacked slid away, crashing into the river with a massive splash.

Noah examined his new blade, stunned at its power.

"When both our minds are at peace and we're able to fully connect, I can transfer more of my power to you. By doing that, together we can overtake any enemy that crosses our path," Lucia said. "You just need to remember that it takes immense concentration and reaction time to use it effectively — both from an Angel and a mortal. If we're not on the same page, things could go very bad."

Noah nodded with his reassuring smile and said, "Okay, I think I understand. So with that settled, there's only one last thing we need to decide on before we head out."

"Oh, and that is…?"

"We need a name for our sword."

Lucia laughed. "Seriously? It's just a sword. Who cares what it's called?"

"What?! No, it's *not* just a sword! It's as much a bond between us as being in unity. It needs to have a proper name." Noah tapped his chin and admired the sword before finally snapping his fingers in excitement. "Oathkeeper!"

"Oathkeeper?"

"Yeah! Remember back in the ruins when I said that as your mortal I would help you rediscover your memories? That was the oath I took to you when we unified, and I intend to keep it. This sword will always act as a reminder to that promise. Oathkeeper."

"Oathkeeper..." Lucia took a moment to grasp how important this name was to Noah, and then agreed. "Okay, Oathkeeper it is."

Noah strapped the blade onto his back. "Great. With that settled, I think it's high time that we set off. But wait...I don't suppose you have a magical map kicking around somewhere, do you?"

Lucia shook her head. "Nope, can't say that I do."

"Well then, I suppose we just start walking. I'm sure we'll find a town or village at some point."

Lucia appreciated his optimism, but she had her doubts. "Don't you think that might be a bad idea? The Engvall army could be searching these jungles for us as we speak."

She had a point, but Noah shook his head. "This didn't really occur to me last night, but I don't think that'll be an issue. We're in the Kerfoot region, and Engvall is part of the Ekholm region. I don't know much about politics, but I do know that a city of a different region bringing their army into another regions land won't go over well. Angel Island is a bit of a grey spot for Kerfoot, but to come chasing us here more in the mainland...it would only cause them more headaches."

That seemed like a fair counterpoint, and so Lucia accepted his logic. She couldn't speak much about Alterra politics either, but she was sure that anything resembling an invasion would *not* go over well.

With their decision set, together they made their way into the jungle with hopes of finding civilization.

Similar to Noah's trip with the army, the jungle was filled with all sorts of feral creatures. The only difference was that they had no clear path to follow, which made for a bit of blind walking.

Along the way, they dealt with creatures like centaspikes—massive insects with mini spikes all over the base of their long, furry bodies. Then there were falcors, which were heavy, black and red birds with talons sharp enough to claw a mortal in half. Most people had zero desire to approach such dangers, but Noah was enjoying himself. It was great practice for him and Lucia to preform unity, and with his newfound power he was feeling particularly invigorated.

The morning heat of Kerfoot beat down on them, and with a full week's worth of battles crammed into only a few hours, the partners stopped for a brief break.

They rested under one of the tall, four-leaf trees that provided plenty of shade while Lucia glanced up, catching glimpses of creatures weaving through the jungle. "I know I've been asleep for a long time, and I certainly don't remember much, but I swear that the creatures in Alterra were never this vicious."

"It never used to be this way," Noah told her. "At least that's what my grandpa said a few years ago. He told me stories about how when he was growing up, they were free to explore almost anywhere without worry. But as Engvall started mining and excavating ether from the planet, I guess things changed. Some animals began to mutate, and over the years it created new breeds of far more vicious monsters rather than scenic wildlife. Then again, that's what ether poisoning can do to someone. It takes even the calmest, docile animal and turns them into a rabid monster."

Lucia did her best to examine the different creatures, the birds in the air, and the rabbits on the ground, and when she did, she could indeed sense something new within them—a trace of ether that mixed with their blood. *This is what ether warfare could cause once again…Wait, why do I remember that? A war…over ether?*

Lucia shook her head, catching Noah's attention. "Hey, are you okay?"

Lucia hesitated, then nodded and stood up. "Yeah, I'm fine. I was just thinking we should get a move on. I'm in desperate need of a real bed tonight."

After a restful break, the two continued trekking along the unmarked paths of the jungle until they finally caught sight of an exit. The thick abundance of trees gradually began to part, and replacing it were long stretches of rolling plains. The hills continued for miles, fresh, green, and filled with wildlife. To the left were winding cliffs that climbed to the sky, while on their right were stone structures that interconnected like bridges, though it was all of natural growth from the lands. Along the coast was the Seraph Sea.

"Phew, I was starting to think we were never going to get out of that jungle," Noah said.

But Lucia was concentrating on something else out into the sea. "Look at that!" But she wasn't interested in the water. Along the Seraph Sea was a series of stone buildings wrapped around a long, granite barrier about ten-feet tall. From the distance it was hard to tell, but it looked like a decent-sized town. Not Engvall levels of metropolis status, but definitely bigger than Berrios by a large margin.

"Well, that's seems like as good a place as any to start if you ask me. Care to head out?" Noah asked.

Lucia agreed, and the two started their way along the vast plains, taking in the sights and sounds of the various creatures. Unlike in the jungle, most of these animals were docile, making their journey quite easy.

The two reached the outer walls of the stone city along the water, and with them came a whole new culture to explore.

On the outside of the walls were two large machines used to move stone slabs into place. An extension was currently being built onto the wall. For what purpose, they couldn't be sure.

Unlike Engvall, these heavy machines were being controlled by people—groups of them, all wearing bright yellow hard hats. Some were directing the workers from below, while others were standing on the top of the wall trying to steady the slabs into place. They were quite cheerful as they did it, laughing and joking with one another. It was a stark contrast to Noah's experience in Engvall.

But there was also something else that Noah was unaccustomed to. Those who were operating the crane looked Human enough, but their skin was a fair bit darker and their noses more pointed, with whiskers like mice.

"Hey, Lucia, are those Angels?"

She examined them and shook her head. "No, definitely not. But I can't say they're Human either." She tried to wrap her brain around any lost memories, but nothing came to mind. She sighed and turned to shrug at Noah, but before she could he was already gone. Darting her head around, she saw him approaching the workers, wearing his signature grin and waving a big hello to them. Before she could stop her naive partner, Noah began chatting up the mousey mortals, and both their and Noah's attentions turned to Lucia. She became flustered, wondering what they were talking about, before they shared a nod and Noah started walking back over to her.

She raised an eyebrow. "So what was that all about?"

"I just asked who they were, where we were, and if there was anywhere we could stay for the night. I don't mind sleeping on the beach, but this way we can get some real rest without worrying about what might be crawling around us."

"You really are something," Lucia said, rolling her eyes with a slight smile. "Anything else you wanna to tell me?"

"Well, this town is called Stone Cutter, and those people aren't Human — they're Ratics. They seem nice enough, at least based on Mowser over there. Anyway, he said we should head for Stone Palace, which is the elder's building, if we're looking for anything related to Angels. I guess there aren't a lot of Angels around here, but the Elder is big on his history so he might have some knowledge we could use."

"You got all that from a stranger…and you believed him?"

Lucia's skepticism was justified, but to Noah it warranted a simple response. "Mowser has no reason to lie. I didn't ask him for money or secret information—I just wanted to know where we were. And even if he *was* lying to us, it's still better than going off of nothing. So I say we head out to find this Elder and see what we can learn."

Lucia said no more and accepted Noah's plan.

All of Stone Cutter was paved with neatly carved cobblestone that veered off in different directions. Though nothing like the infrastructure of Engvall, it was actually rather similar to Berrios. Each path led to a different part of the town and, as the name indicated, everything was finely crafted out of stone. Shops, inns, houses—all of them different shapes and sizes but confined to the stone their town was built with.

At the north end was a structure that put the rest to shame. The markings in the rock had strange symbols and a few emblems, and the rock's height towered over the rest of Stone Cutter. It certainly stood out as a place of importance.

"Ratics are quite a handy group of people, aren't they? Imagine building all this…and it looks like they're barely using any ether to do it."

"I just hope their beds aren't made out of stone too," Lucia quipped.

They tried to keep on task, but Noah couldn't help take a peek at the pop-up shops that were all around. It was like a whole new world for him, and he was fascinated by it.

Like Noah had assumed, Ratics were great at crafting. And it wasn't limited to stone crafting, either. As they walked through the entrance of town, Noah spotted clothing stores with all kinds of knitted wears, and various tool shops for different projects. He could feel a rich history around him, one that dated back centuries, and despite his mission he wanted to learn about it. He was quite like his grandpa when it came to new things.

On the other hand, with Noah lost in curiosity, Lucia continued to feel strange. With every step they took, she could feel everyone's eyes fixated on her. When she moved, so did they. Was it because she was an Angel? They'd yet to see other Angels around, so it made sense that they'd be intrigued. Perhaps Angels were a rare sight around Stone Cutter.

But no, they didn't feel like eyes of intrigue. These people didn't display an ounce of curiosity, unlike her partner at the moment. These were eyes of worry, and it made the air tense. Nobody said a word to them, but the constant whispers were definitely audible, though faintly.

The closer they got to Stone Palace, the commotion in the streets began to intensify. People were starting to back away from Lucia and Noah, while others stopped what they were doing to cautiously observe them. Some even slipped into nearby stores to hide. The tension in the air only grew thicker.

Finally, Lucia said, "Noah, I don't think we're exactly welcome here."

"What do you mean?" Confused, Noah followed her gaze until he spotted a group of soldiers marching down the street. They were far less imposing than any Engvall soldier, their gear much more on par with Noah's, but their spears were still sharp. Behind them, he noticed a pair of Angels with even more intimidating glares. This was definitely concerning.

It wasn't just from the direction of the palace the soldiers were marching. From all four of the various pathways walked different groups, some with heavier armor, some with swords, and a few drawing their bows. They all had one thing in common — their eyes were locked on Noah.

No, it wasn't Noah they were eying. It was Lucia.

"I have a bad feeling about this…" she whispered.

The guards surrounded them, and a decorated woman separated from the group. Sown onto her chest were a few different badges with strange markings on them.

She brandished her spear, and ordered, "Drop your weapons and put your hands up, Angel of Death!"

There was that name again, the same one Bower had called her. Angel of Death. Lucia flinched, unsure what to do.

"Angel of Death? What are you talking about?" Noah looked to the guard, then to Lucia and then back to the guard. "Are you talking about Lucia? She's no Angel of Death." His face became cross, offended at the treatment of his Angel.

The other soldiers moved in and the guard captain said, "I don't care what you think her name is, kid. Now step aside and comply. Our business is with the monster behind you."

Noah's voice became more defensive as he took a step back, bumping into Lucia. "She's not a monster! I don't know anything about this 'Angel of Death' you're talking about, but you've got the wrong Angel.

"Noah…I'd do what they say," Lucia whispered.

A split hesitation, then Noah stopped and said, "This

has to be some sort of misunderstanding. I'm telling you—you guys have the wrong Angel."

"Oh, we don't have the wrong Angel. She bares the symbol of the Arch Angel, the holy wings. I don't know what she's got you believing, but she is nothing more than a weapon for destruction. Now step aside, kid. I don't want to hurt you."

"I said no," Noah repeated firmly.

But Lucia shook her head. "Thank you, Noah, but that's enough. Whatever it is they're talking about, I can handle this myself. I know they can't harm me. That said, they can harm *you*. And even with my power, there are far too many guards to fight our way out of this. The best course of action is to listen to them and talk this out."

Lucia didn't like what she was saying any more than Noah did, but clearly there was something going on, and seemingly more than just the Engvall army wanting her. This was the only thing she could think of to keep Noah safe.

Noah grabbed his sword, his mind still running through scenarios. He glanced to his left and saw soldiers, then to his right where he saw them again. He side-eyed Lucia, who remained poised, and then he sighed. He tossed his weapon to his left, and it clanked off the stone before landing defeatedly a few feet in front of the guard captain.

Unarmed, the guards moved in. They grabbed Lucia's arms, put them behind her back, and slapped on a pair of glowing handcuffs. An ether suppression device. It would never contain her full power, or most Angels' power for that matter. It would, however, drain them to the point of not being able to fight for very long.

Noah, on the other hand, faced a less dignified arrest. A kick to the back of his leg dropped him to his knees before he was shoved to the ground.

"Hey!" Lucia shouted. "We're doing what you ordered, so don't you dare hurt him!"

The guard captain turned back to look at the fiery Angel. "Easy there, Angel of Death. We won't rough him up too much, just as long as you choose to co-operate."

"Excuse me! I'm an Angel, and if I wasn't co-operating, you would know it," she barked back. Her antics were drawing the attention of the soldiers around them, but then they saw Noah lift his head.

"It's okay, Lucia. I'm fine. It's like you said, we'll figure this out. It's clearly all one big misunderstanding." Noah got to his knees, a smear of dirt on his face and a thin cut on his cheek. He tried to smile as handcuffs were clenched around his wrists.

Two soldiers lifted Noah to his feet and started walking him east, while the rest of the group surrounded Lucia and escorted her to the palace. She tried to look over to Noah in the distance.

I'm sorry, Noah...

CHAPTER 8
A LEGACY UNWANTED

Even after the commotion had settled down, Lucia remained hot. She knew she was safe—even from a basic observation she could tell that the guards were no match for her. That was without Noah around, either. On the other hand, the same could not be said of Noah without her by his side. He was at their mercy, and that tied her stomach in knots.

If there was any kind of a bright side to all this, Lucia had been marched straight into Stone Palace.

The palace walls were like granite, sparkling and shining from the different coloured gemstones encased underneath. She stood in a long, elegant hallway with pillars that had various historical people carved into them, not that Lucia could recall any of them. A black carpet ran through the middle of the hall before veering off onto two different paths.

After being trudged down the hall, she finally reached a stone door. She was surprised to hear the guards who'd followed her saying, "The Elder will be with you in a moment."

They were positioned directly behind her, and she could feel their peering eyes fixated on her—but specifically her hands, which were under lock and key with glowing handcuffs. The light pulsing through them emitted a strange, almost intoxicating sensation that Lucia felt through her body. She assumed they were suppressing the ether in her blood somehow in order to weaken her.

She could also sense the growing unease of those around her. Their breathing was tight and their bodies tense, as though they were waiting for her to strike out in rage. They knew as well as she did that the handcuffs would be nothing but a road bump for her if she were to choose.

"You know, it's rude to stare..." she blithely shot at them. The guards bolted upright upon hearing her taunt.

"Look, I'm not interested in attacking anyone here, so as long as you don't hurt the kid, then we won't have any problems. Got it?"

The guards said nothing and continued waiting.

Lucia took those moments to gather her thoughts. She'd once again been called the Angel of Death, which by no means was a compliment. Everyone was always on edge whenever she showed herself, which was tough enough to deal with, but with no context as to why they were calling her such a name, defending herself was even more of a struggle. She wanted to speak to the Elder of Stone Cutter and gather some more information, but to do so she'd have to be on her best behavior—even if it meant excusing their mistreatment of Noah by throwing him in jail with no crime committed.

The wait was growing tiresome, but soon Lucia heard someone walking from down the hall. Now it was her turn to tighten up, her breath catching in her chest. She tried to hide any signs of anxiety before realizing it wasn't the Elder heading in her direction.

The person walking toward them was in fact not a person at all, at least based on the glowing, blue eyes. She was an Angel, but a friendly one, it seemed. She was dressed elegantly, though in no way did she exhibit the fighting prowess of Lucia. Her teal hair flowed down her back in curls, and her smile was warm and comforting.

Lucia heard the armour behind her clank as the two guards took a bow.

"Greetings, Lady Ophelia. We are honoured." Their words had the utmost of formality to them. Lucia assumed this was the Angel of the Elder. It was the only explanation.

A feeling of grace filled the room as Ophelia approached them, and that grace was evident in the words she spoke as well.

"Thank you, gentlemen. We appreciate you bringing our guest to us. I shall take things from here. You are both dismissed."

The guards raised their heads from their bowing position and saluted before leaving the room.

Lucia locked eyes with Ophelia. It was just the two of them left in the room. She was hopeful there was some sort of kinship given the fact that they were both Angels, but Lady Ophelia dispelled that quickly.

"So, you are the Arch Angel Lucia…or should I call you the Angel of Death?"

Lucia tensed, fighting to keep her tone measured. "No, I'd rather you not call me that. And frankly, I'd appreciate it if everyone else stopped as well. I don't even know where that name came from."

Ophelia seemed puzzled, but then nodded. "All right… Lucia. Regardless, I wish to thank you for coming to see the Elder. He has a lot he would like to discuss with you."

"It's not like I had much of a choice—your soldiers threw my mortal in jail and dragged me here."

"Ah, yes, I suppose this is true." There was some slight remorse in Ophelia's words. "I do apologize for any undo suffering these events have caused. But you must understand—people around here harbour great trepidation at the sight of the Angel of Death. It is very unsettling."

Lucia was visibly frustrated, and Ophelia quickly backtracked. "My apologies. I didn't mean to insinuate—"

"Can you just show me to the Elder? I'd like to get this mess cleared up as soon as possible and get Noah out of jail."

"Right, of course. Please follow me." Ophelia guided Lucia down the right path of the hall.

The walk was silent, and Lucia felt somewhat poorly for the way she spoke to Ophelia. The two didn't know each other, and she was just relaying the information presented to her, which was evident by Ophelia's apology. Lucia thought about apologizing herself, but she remained quiet, figuring it was best to just leave things alone.

Up a flight of stairs they went and then down another winding hall. At the end of the second floor was a mammoth door, decorated with all sorts of different gemstones. There was a solider on the left and an Angel on the right, both wearing Stone Cutter insignias on their armour. They bowed to Ophelia as she approached, then pushed the doors open.

The next room was ornately decorated, displaying a great linage. In the back was a long window that stretched across half of the wall. The clouds were beginning to creep in outside, but there was still a tremendous view of the town below them through the windows. That's where Lucia saw a short man with his arms behind his back, gazing upon his town.

"Elder," Ophelia said to the man, "as you requested, I have brought Lucia here to speak with you."

The Elder slowly turned to place his eyes on Lucia. His face was far more weathered than Lucia had expected, and his body had a pronounced hunch. He wore a black and white robe that draped off his skinny arms. The way he walked made his old age evident, and he made no effort to pick up his pace. When he spoke, it was slow and refined like a man of great wisdom.

"Thank you, Ophelia, it is much appreciated." He slowly walked over to the stone desk in the middle of the room, picking up a piece of paper and handing it to her. "If you don't mind, could you also pick up some supplies for me? I'll handle things from here."

Ophelia accepted his orders without debate and left the room, and what remained was thick tension. The Elder stared at Lucia just as everyone else had, but unlike their reactions, his face twisted in confusion. He locked onto the stone Angel wings on her chest. There was no mistaking the wings of the Arch Angel. "That emblem, the soul stone of the Arch Angel…so it is true then—you have returned from your slumber. I'd heard rumors of the Engvall Empire attempting to find you, but I believed it to be nothing more than a myth."

"I can assure you, I'm no myth," Lucia said, grudgingly.

"And yet you look quite different from the tales of history. Is this a new form of yours?"

"I'm sorry? This is the form I've always had."

"Hmm…" The elder stroked his chin, and then, "Perhaps history was mistaken. Regardless, where are my manners? Allow me to introduce myself. I am Elder Adidas Amrust, the leader of Stone Cutter. It is truly an honour to meet you." He took a formal bow, his robes traipsing along the ground.

But Lucia was less than impressed by his etiquette. She was fuming but still tried to control herself, though it was difficult. "Your guards have been calling me the Angel of Death since I stepped foot in this place, and you threw my mortal in your jail without any formal charges of a crime. The only reason I'm here is to demand his release." The subtle anger in her voice was not to be played with, and Elder Adidas understood that.

"Please, do accept my apologies. It is not custom for the Stone Cutter people to treat foreigners with such hostilities. This is a hardworking town, open to anyone willing to put in a little elbow grease, so please do not take your anger out on them. The arrest of your mortal was my doing, but when I heard news of your return, I was forced to take precautions. I'm sure that you of all people understand why I had to separate you from your mortal?"

"Because an Angel's power is severely limited without

their ability to achieve unity. I'm aware, though I must admit that these ether-absorbing handcuffs you slapped on me were unexpected." Lucia paused to let her anger simmer a little before speaking in a more acceptable tone. "Regardless of who gave the orders, was that truly necessary? He's just a kid, after all. He didn't even mean to bond with me in the first place—it was honestly dumb luck on his part. If you've got a bone to pick with me, that's fine. But he doesn't deserve to be punished."

"That is rather compassionate of you to show such care to a mortal—especially one you say unified with you out of 'dumb luck,' as you put it. But I disagree. I believe our actions were justified. With that said, you do have my word as the Elder of Stone Cutter that no harm will be brought to him. As you pointed out, he has done nothing wrong, and I would never allow punishment of the innocent. But the people of Stone Cutter are my first responsibility, and after the way you left our fair town, it was a necessity."

Lucia's tendency to retort gave way to a new emotion—guilt. She was scared to ask, but she knew that she needed to. "What do you mean...how I left your town?"

Adidas scrutinized her words, refusing to be played for a fool, but he was also a good judge of character. Though there was no mistaking the emblem representing the Arch Angel, there was no sign of a liar, either.

Lucia picked up on this and decided to speak before he could ask further questions. "Look. For what it's worth, I've only been awake for a day and I don't have any recollection of my memories." Her voice became softer, her vitriol melting away. "So I'm sorry if I did anything to you, your family, or this place in the past...but even so, Noah had nothing to do with it, nor did he intend to awaken me. If you have issues with me, I understand, but the only reason I came here was to request that you let him go."

"I see. In that case, I believe we can reach an agreement regarding the arrest of…Noah is his name? We will set Noah free, assuming your next few answers are acceptable."

"That's fine. But remember, I don't have any memories of the past. I'll do my best, but I can't make any promises."

"That will be acceptable. First, I want to know why you have returned to Stone Cutter. What is it that you seek from us?"

"That's simple enough to answer. As you already know, the Engvall army came hunting me down. They tried to take me and kill Noah, but we managed a lucky escape. Since I had no memories, Noah said he would help me learn about my past…help me regain my memories. We wandered our way here after escaping Engvall. That's all—I didn't come to cause destruction or death or anything like that."

"I see," Elder Adidas said, thinking carefully. "This brings up another issue that I believe will need to be taken care of with Engvall. However, to say I am surprised by their lust for power would be a lie." The Elder walked over to the window gazing down on his beloved town, gesturing for Lucia to come as well.

"As I was born long after your time, I cannot provide you with the memories you seek. However, allow me to present you with a brief history lesson. It is knowledge that has been continuously passed down through the years—although I must warn you, it will not be easy to hear."

Lucia joined him at the window, staring over the water

and the houses below. She swallowed hard, balancing her desire to remember against her fear of knowing. But she knew that ignoring history would lead her to repeat it. "I can handle it. I want to know."

"All right," the Elder nodded. "The last time you were awake was over 300 years ago, in a time period known as the Angel Wars. The phenomena known as Angels and soul stones were quite new, and people around Alterra were only just beginning to discover the blessings you Angels possessed. But in time, those strengths were gradually used to gain power — particularly when it came down to rations and supplies. As you have already experienced I'm sure, Engvall — a growing metropolis at the time — was learning to harness ether in ways that nobody else could begin to imagine. Those accomplishments, although greatly enhancing the lives of many, also allowed them to take their weapons and spread their might outward. That's when the war started. Angels and their mortals were thrust into great battles, with much bloodshed and hardship. This fight would continue for years, with every region across the Seraph Sea at each other's throats. Mostly, however, Engvall and Solace of the Drake region. Engvall was gathering up anyone who had united with their Angel and killed them, collecting their soul stone in hopes of using their ether to maintain their Empire. It was a never-ending battle, until one day years into the fray, a group of new Angels appeared. They were powerful beyond compare, even carrying multiple blessing within them. And amongst those were two Angels known as the Arch Angels. They were a gift from the Guardian Angel to end the war, and their soul stones were in the shape of Angel wings—one in blue and one in red. However, everywhere these two went, destruction followed at an unprecedented rate."

He paused, and Lucia's heart raced as she prepared for what was to come.

He continued, "As I am sure you have figured out, you were one of those Angels. You possessed a power unlike anything Alterra had ever seen before. Though I'm not so naive to believe how or why rumors grow, history says that where you went, death followed. This is why history gave you the name Angel of Death. Stone Cutter is a peaceful town but, being on the water, it was also a good invasion point for Engvall to make tracks inside the Kerfoot region. The stories say that you passed through this humble town, and in an hour there was nothing left. It was leveled into oblivion, killing nearly everyone within the town as well. That is why to this day the people here fear your return. They simply wish not to be caught in your path of destruction again."

Lucia took a step back, the colour in her face all but drained. She stared down at her feet, speechless. She was a cold-hearted killer of an Angel—someone that had left a bloody mark on history.

"How…how did it end…?" Lucia finally stammered.

"That part is a bit murky, but it is said that shortly after, there was a battle between the two Arch Angels. And when it was over, Engvall ceased their war, brokering a peace treaty that still exists to this day. But the Arch Angels were said to have disappeared shortly after, leaving us with only stories to tell."

Lucia took a deep breath, trying to regain her composure. "I see. I know my words don't count for much, and they'll never bring back the lives that I've stolen or the families I've ripped apart in the past, but I do sincerely apologize for my actions."

"Your words hold truth, Arch Angel. I can see you are not as they have described you. But as for the people of Stone Cutter, I cannot speak for them or their forgiveness. Many generations of families continued to live here long after the rebuild, and they know the damage that was caused."

"I understand. So allow me to put the people of Stone Cutter at ease. Release my mortal and we'll be on our way. We won't spend a night at the inn, we won't say a word of our arrival, and we'll leave without a whisper. You have my word as the Arch Angel of Alterra."

Elder Adidas took the time to consider Lucia's words, and replied with a somber smile. He didn't appear to feel any malice toward the Angel, despite her history. Perhaps it was because they were talking in person, and he could see her sincere nature. Still, Lucia understood that he was doing what was best for his people, and for that she could respect his leadership.

"I believe that would be a fair trade." Elder Adidas walked over to his desk and grabbed a piece of paper. He pulled out some ink and jotted down a note before calling in one of the guards.

"Adamis, please take this note to the jail and request release of the boy named Noah. Then escort him and our Arch Angel here out of town." He handed the note to the guard, Adamis, and turned his attention back to Lucia for one last word of warning. "I am taking you at your word,

Arch Angel. But if you are to play me for a fool, I assure you that our forces will not look favorably upon you or that boy. Do not let me down."

"I can assure you that I'm not playing anybody. As long as you keep your word, I'll be gone. Promise." Lucia raised her arms up revealing the shackles, blinking with the green light of ether. Her hands and wrists started glowing near flawless white, and with a quick twitch she was able to snap the shackles off. She'd had the power to do so all along.

The guard reached for his lance, preparing to protect Elder Adidas, but Elder Adidas' face presented no signs of worry, and the guard was again at ease. The Elder and Lucia both knew that with Noah in the dungeons, there was no room for violence.

"So you were just humouring our technology, it appears. Even without a mortal to unite with, the ether in you appears to be unmatched by any Angel we've come across. I shall take this as a sign that you were only allowing yourself to be cuffed to mitigate the fear that you'd already caused?"

Lucia agreed. "Now please just let Noah go. And, like I said, we'll be on our way."

Elder Adidas gestured for the guard to leave. Lucia was about to follow behind him but before they could depart, Ophelia burst through the doors. Her face was unusually pale, and her hair a mess as though she'd just been in a full sprint.

In the distance, explosions started going off, and faint cries of terror soon followed.

"Sir, we're under attack!" Ophelia cried.

"Is it the Engvall army?" Lucia responded.

"No, it's two Angels, but they appear to be alone. No uniteds around them."

All eyes were fixed on Lucia, their stares of judgment unrelenting.

"I'm not sure why you're looking at me! Why don't you get your guards and defend those people you care so much about?" Her bark was slightly vicious, and under most circumstances talking to authority in such a voice would be ill advised, but she made a compelling argument.

The guard and Ophelia waited for the Elder to officially give his orders. "The Arch Angel is right — our priority is defending the town. Inform the guard captain and tell her to get all citizens to safety. Bring them to the palace, if need be. We can shelter anyone we must." The Elder turned his concentrated gaze to Lucia. "Are you ready to prove your sincerity?"

"Release Noah and then yes — I'll deal with these Angels."

"Very well." Elder Adidas grabbed the note from the guard and handed it to Ophelia. "Head to the jail and release the boy named Noah right away."

Ophelia nodded and everyone took off down the halls of the palace and then outside. As they did, a massive shadow gradually engulfed the palace. Propellers sputtered loudly from overhead, and Lucia and the Elder glanced up.

"Whoa...it's huge!" Lucia gawked. High above them bloating out the sky was a colossal airship, nearly the size of a small town itself. Pulsating green lights ran through it, and the body was encased in impenetrable steel armour.

"Leviathan," Adidas said grimly.

"Leviathan? That sounds bad."

"History says that it was destroyed in the Angel Wars by one of the Arch Angels. I don't know who could've restored it to working order. We need to hurry—I fear this is no ordinary foe."

"I'll go on ahead!" Lucia took off down the winding path from the palace into the crux of Stone Cutter. Running perpendicular to her was a battalion of guards, but this time they showed no interest in stopping her. Their focus lay on the airship Leviathan that moved ominously from the palace over the city.

The foul stench of tyranny wafted through the streets as Lucia followed the guards. She cast her arm to the side, and strings of light danced until Oathkeeper appeared before her; luckily, an Angel could upon call their weapon at any time. Unfortunately, the drawback was that Noah, who had been in possession of their shared weapon, would be left with nothing to defend himself. He'd also have no way of calling it back.

That said, Lucia weighed the odds, and she figured for the time being that it would be a safe assumption that if Noah was in a dungeon, there was no way the guards would let him keep their sword. Even that goofy smile of his couldn't talk his way into such an obvious mistake.

For Angels, there was one scenario in which they couldn't call their weapons back, but it would involve being unified with Noah, and that wasn't about to happen.

When she reached the town center, she was stunned at what she saw. Through the streets, waves of people from Angels to Ratics to Humans were all running in the opposite direction. Guards waved their arms like traffic cops trying to usher anyone within sight to make an escape.

The shadow of Leviathan absorbed the light of Stone Cutter as it blocked out the sun. Lucia could see metal hatches on the bottom of the ship that looked like tiles. They were creaking open, and from the black voids inside rained a handful of Angels, sinking like rockets until they crashed into the ground, causing earthquakes.

Lucia raised her blade, the light forming in the middle as she braced for a fight. Around her, everyone who'd been fleeing for their lives slowed to catch a glimpse of the Arch Angel that had previously terrified them. They were stunned that she was about to take up arms in their stead.

"I'll handle these guys! Get yourselves to safety!" she yelled to the guards.

"Why should we trust you?!" one of them rebutted.

"Because I'm your best chance of living right now!" Her fiery orders compelled the guards to take her word. Besides, she'd made a valid argument.

With people finally clearing out, Lucia turned her attention to the Angels raining down from the sky. She focused on them and then realized something strange. Their eyes lacked the same spark that all Angels had. And the markings on their bodies were all the same, something extraordinarily rare amongst Angels. She was staring at a group of clones. Lanky, with greyish-black skin, and astonishingly expressionless faces.

"Who are you guys!?" she shouted, but the strange "Angels" only responded with a menacing grunt. In unison, they raised their left hands, and weapons formed.

To Lucia's right, echoes of steel clashed in a violent battle.

She split her focus to take a brief glance and saw a group of guards holding off the same type of Angels who stood in front of her. The sheer number of clones was enough of an indication that though they looked like Angels, and perhaps even carried some of the same blessings, they were nothing but fakes. But the guards were struggling, and ether blasts were being shaken off by the fake Angels with relative ease. Lucia knew she'd be forced to fight with whatever strength she could summon in return.

The group of fake Angels in front of Lucia started making more sounds, and the one in front, holding a thin, steel samurai sword, grunted out unintelligible words. This time, it sounded like an order, and the fake Angels behind the leader began charging forward.

Lucia leapt back, distancing herself from the enemy. She watched their movements to gauge their speed. Three clones launched their attacks from the front with two charging from the sides—all of them attempting to skewer her.

Turning to the defensive, Lucia, through the one power of her blessing that she could recall, cast up her barrier and created a transparent oval shield that encased her body. The weapons clanked off her as though they were smacking into a wall, and with a grunt of her own she cast her hands forward. The shield burst outward, sending a shockwave that shoved the fakes back. "So you guys want to play hard ball?! Fine with me!" she shouted through a few deep breaths. There was no question that using her blessings still caused a great strain, and turning it into an outward attack was even more of a burden, but it was nothing she wasn't prepared to handle.

Gripping Oathkeeper, she began whipping it back and

forth, shooting out long, arching beams of light. The attacks were met by the defenses of each clone's weapons, but the sheer power managed to stagger them. Lucia flew forward with the grace befitting her Arch Angel status and swung with a ferocity that left the fake Angels stunned and back peddling as they defended. She was relentless, proving her strength with quickness and power until she beat the fakes into submission. With one final slash she dropped all five of the Angels to the ground, leaving them slumped over before their bodies exploded into small, green particles. Nothing remained of the decaying bodies, but the particles rose to the sky, returning to Leviathan. *What is going on here?*

She easily confirmed her earlier assumption that these were indeed fakes. When Angels received critical damage, they'd revert back to their soul stone forms before losing their light. They wouldn't dissolve into particles, looking like ether and floating through the air.

Though determining the source of these fakes would be important in time, she had to remain focused on her task. There was still plenty of danger present.

With the weaker fakes now disposed of, a blast of fire ripped through the air in Lucia's direction. With fractions of a second to react, she repeated casting her dome of light to absorb the impact. Though the impact sent shockwaves through her body, she sucked up the pain and directed her focus on the surprise attackers.

"That's one hell of a reaction time, but I guess I shouldn't be all that surprised. The power of the Arch Angel really is a beauty to behold." The voice Lucia heard was confident—arrogant, even.

Through the smoke and embers, Lucia spotted two shadows emerging. One was tall, thin, and with a yellowish blond hair — kind of resembling a pop star from Earth. He carried his sword like an accessory, and his walk was full of flamboyancy. Beside him was a short, stout girl with a hammer that matched her size. It didn't look possible for such a small frame to lift that heavy a weapon, but she flung it around with ease. Her long hair flew around her eyes, which were glowing bright red.

Those are real Angels. Are they the ones who restored Leviathan?

Lucia focused herself and pointed her blade in the direction of her new enemies. "Who are you two, and why are you attacking these people?"

The pair of Angels kept walking closer, both with sickening grins on their faces. The girl spoke first. "Don't flatter them, Arch Angel — we've got no business with this place. We just want *you*," she sniveled, dropping her hammer on the ground and cracking the stone walkway underneath.

"Now now, Petra. There's no need to be so rude to our dear Angel — she's just reawakened, after all. Please allow me to introduce ourselves. We are agents of Alterra. I am the great Marco, and this little ray of sunshine is Petra. And might I say, my dear Arch Angel, only someone of your elegance could hold such beauty."

"Can it, lover boy," Lucia seethed.

"Oh, and I see that your tongue is as sharp as ever. Most would find such language unbecoming from an Angel of your stature, but not I. I dare say it's quite attractive," Macro chided.

Lucia's face scrunched in frustration. "You think my tongue is sharp? Just wait until you see the edge of blade! Now what do you want with me?!"

"My dear, we have simply come to retrieve you so that you may fulfill your duty as the Arch Angel."

"My duty as the Arch Angel?" She caught a glimpse of Leviathan gliding overhead, its shadow of doom overtaking them once again. She put aside any questions about her duty and said, "And what makes you think I want anything to do with you? Angels going around attacking mortals with no regard for life aren't exactly Angels I care to join."

"We thought you might say that," Petra snarled, "so here are your options. Come quietly with us and we can leave with minimal bloodshed, or we bring this whole place crumbling down and take you by force." She raised her hammer with both hands. The markings on the face of the hammer looked familiar to Lucia, but her memory refused to recall them.

Petra didn't bother waiting for an answer, instead smashing her hammer down on the stone. Waves of spikes jetted up along the ground and rampaged toward Lucia.

Countering with ease, Lucia swung her sword wide and the beam of light blasted out, slicing the tops of the rocks like bread. Such skill should've brought a glimmer of hope, but Lucia knew that her victory was far from assured. There was still heavy danger in the air. She glanced up following her senses and, looking every bit like the Angel he was, Marco soared through the air. Thanks to the incredible length of his sword, he was on top of Lucia well before he was even close. She raised her sword, blocking the barrage of slashes and sending sparks in every direction.

"Your speed is only matched by your timeless style," Marco said poetically. Lucia couldn't determine the difference between his obnoxious flirting and his incessant mocking.

She thrust her sword forward but continued to miss. She jumped back, then shouted "Halo slash!" and fired off rings of light in succession.

Marco once again lifted his slender, long sword and blocked her efforts. Instead of exploding on contact, they sailed around Marco and into the sky or down to the ground.

Lucia noticed something strange about her attacks. As they got closer to Marco, it was like they were hitting a force of wind that slowed down the beams before reaching an invisible force field that repelled them for good.

There's no way he's this fast. It must be his blessing…but how does it work? She was fixated on the cause. In need of information, Lucia decided to keep Marco at bay and focus on Petra. She assumed that the diminutive Angel could create waves of spikes through her hammer. At least her ability was straightforward. Dangerous if one wasn't cautious, but much more physical in nature.

Strategically, Lucia fired off another round of halo slashes at Petra, who was only a few feet away from Marco. She knew the attack was no threat, but she wanted to see what Marco would do. To her surprise, her hunch carried more weight than expected—Marco raised his sword and the tip of the blade stretched past Petra's torso. Just like before, the rings of light repelled like magnets and crashed into the ground, sending up smoke and debris.

Neither of them even tried to get out of the way, so Marco's blessing must be some sort of ether repellent. That's gonna make this an issue when he combines it with the reach of his sword. And Petra's ability to send stone spikes is a huge advantage. Damn it.

"You figure it out yet?" Marco mockingly called out as the smoke disappeared from their battlefield.

If there was anything Lucia refused to show, it was fear. She lacked memories, but she was still the Arch Angel of Alterra, and that came with a level of expectation. She gripped Oathkeeper and smirked, "Yeah, I think I did. I'm not sure on the specifics, but your blessing is repelling ether. And the reason you use such a long sword is because the blade is what's actually the repellent."

"Beauty *and* smarts! You really are the whole package, aren't you? You're right—I can repel ether with the tip of my blade. Our blessings can come in all shapes and forms, and though mine might not allow for any physical dominance like some others, I assure you it's more than useful."

Lucia gritted her teeth. She took a quick glance to check her surroundings before realizing that nobody else was around. They'd all managed to escape, not that it would matter if she couldn't hold off the agents of Alterra here. *What's taking them so long to release Noah?!*

Once again Marco soared through the sky, setting his sights on Lucia while Petra slammed her hammer on the ground, rocking the very foundation of Stone Cutter.

"Is that really the best the Arch Angel has? Surely you can do better than this!" Marco goaded. His tone became harsher and more manipulative as he continued, "Or is it that you're scared? You fear using that power stored away in you, is that it? You know, if you use your full power, not only will you obliterate this town but also every last living soul in it, and you wouldn't want that on your conscience, now would you?"

The words caused Lucia to flinch and miss the block of Marco's attack. Luckily with her reaction time, she managed to summon her barrier, blocking the strike that landed only inches from her heart. Still, she skidded back, the near-death experience forcing her to catch her breath.

"All you have to do is come quietly and we can call it a day," Petra said from behind them.

Thoughts of Lucia's talk with the Elder came flooding back. The recollection of Stone Cutters history and the damage she'd caused in the past. She hated to see it repeated, even if this time it wasn't by her own hand.

Lowering her sword to her side, Lucia said, "Who is it that sent you here? Who is it that wants to meet me so bad?"

Marco smirked, "Finally, we're starting to get through to you. It's an old friend you might recall by the name of Oberon."

Lucia gasped and a flood of anger filled her. The memories remained a mystery, but just the mention of the name Oberon was enough to trigger a violent reaction.

"So you do remember? He's eager to see you, so get ready."

CHAPTER 9
ONE OF A KIND

Smog filled the air, which grew colder as Noah walked down the tunnels. If he had the power to rub his arms warm, he would've, but the cuffs locking his hands denied such a luxury.

Two guards continued to escort him through what he could only assume were the tunnels leading to the dungeons.

When he was escorted away from Lucia, he'd been taken down a strange route where the civilization of Stone Cutter disappeared. The dungeons weren't located in the crux of the town, but rather in a small subsection just off the outskirts. There was only one way in and one way out, which made monitoring the dungeons easier. But the dungeons weren't often used, something the folks of Stone Cutter were quite proud of. Only a handful of people resided in the jails at one time, and their jails were far from heavily secured. Nothing like in Engvall.

Along the way, Noah repeatedly pled his case, but the guards not only ignored his vocal arguments—they didn't even bother acknowledging them.

But it was strange. Even as he walked unarmed, the guards behind him with spears, he never felt a sense of danger. Perhaps it was because he wasn't the real target in their arrest. That distinction went to Lucia, who he was more worried about than himself. But he needed to have faith. Lucia could handle herself, and so his priority was to not cause her any trouble by being a bad inmate.

There was so much of Stone Cutter's architecture that was a marvel, but the dungeons were far from a masterpiece. The walls were plain, smooth rock and lacked any of the intricacies like in the rest of the town. The path was lit by torches, not ether lights, which Noah found strange. Water seeped through the walls with constant drips, which sounded far louder than they should.

Not that Noah ever thought that he'd wind up in jail, but he did imagine the place to have more security. Each cell only housed a few criminals. And even when Noah looked into the cells, the people in there were far from what he expected. They just looked like drifters, no hardened violence in their eyes. They didn't seem like bad people, at least that's what he believed.

At the end of the hall was the final cell, and as they got closer, he could hear a faint tune being played. It was melodramatic, to say the least.

One of the guards stepped past Noah and grabbed a pair of keys before opening the cell door, which wailed with a heavy grind. There was a single light dangling from the ceiling, and it barely covered one third of the cell. On the left and right sides were basic cots built into the walls. They looked like blocks of cement with a pillow.

When the door opened, Noah heard a voice from the shadows.

"Finally…my fur was in a good need of brushing." The voice was far from intimidating, and sounded as though it had no business being in a jail. Noah could see a small creature sitting in the shadows of the cell.

Out from the corner of the room stepped a small, bi-pedal creature. Its fur was a fluffy and light grey, though there were blobs of dirt on it. The creature's underbelly was a large pale oval, and wrapped around its neck was a rugged, blue-hooded cape. He was holding a harmoni-ca — an instrument Noah could recall Izzy playing once — and he placed it in the pocket of a sash that wrapped from his shoulder and down around his waist.

In the light, Noah realized that the creature was noth-ing more than a small bear with round eyes and a button nose. There was nothing imposing about it at all.

The guard rolled his eyes and said, "Can it, fur ball. You're not going anywhere. And cut it out with the har-monica — you're bugging the other inmates."

The bear cub bellowed, "This travesty won't stand! Don't you know who I am?"

"No, and I don't care." The guard pushed Noah into the cell. "Here's your new cellmate. He's *your* problem now." The door slammed shut and off the guard went.

Noah turned around and stared through the bars of his new home, watching as the guards disappeared around the corner. He could only hope that Lucia was having bet-ter luck than he was.

"So what'd they get you for, friend?" the creature asked.

Noah spun around, forced to look down to his feet so he could see the diminutive bear. When the flicker of the fires shined on his new cellmate, Noah finally realized what he was staring at. "Wait…you're an Ursula, aren't you?"

The bear blinked twice, then tilted his head before stroking the fur of his chin. "Well, look at that—answering my question with another question. All right, I can play this game. What's a united doing in a Stone Cutter jail?"

"Wait, how did you know I was united?"

"That shiny ring on your finger, my friend—that's no ordinary ring. That's a sure sign of someone who's ascended with an Angel, if I do say so myself."

Noah paused. *Right…I guess that's how they knew I was in unity with Lucia.*

The bear pulled him from his thoughts once again. "But that does beg a question…here you are alone, that's unusually suspicious." The Ursula waddled over to the cot on the left side of the room and grabbed the top of the bed, struggling his way upward. He muttered in frustration until he felt his body become weightless. Noah lifted him up and placed him on the bed.

The Ursula crossed his arms. "Thank you kindly. These beds aren't Ursula friendly." Then he turned to fix his eyes on Noah and clapped his paws together. "I've got it. You're in here for killing your Angel, is that it?"

"What?! No!" Noah gawked. "I'd never do that. I'm just in here because of a misunderstanding. I'll be out before the end of the day once this is all cleared up."

"Hmmm, I see. Well, I do believe that could be a possibility…"

Finally, Noah took a moment to reset, and he stuck his hand out with a friendly smile. "I don't know why you're in here, but you seem like a nice Ursula, so I think we should start over. I'm Noah. It's nice to meet you."

"Well, Sir Noah, it's nice to meet you, too. I go by many names, but you may call me Koda. Koda the Adventurer, to be precise. Perhaps you've heard of my many daring and fabulous tales?"

Noah was silent.

"Well, not to worry," Koda continued. "All of it'll soon be documented in my future, number-one-selling book, *Koda the Adventurer, The Greatest Adventurer in the History of Alterra*. You can say that you knew me before I hit the big time, Sir Noah."

Koda posed gallantly in the most heroic way he could.

"Uh…not to be rude, Koda, but you don't look like much of an adventurer to me. Also, I thought that all Ursulas lived in seclusion from the rest of Alterra?"

Koda gasped dramatically, grabbing his cape and waving it around like a spoiled princess. "Not an adventurer, my good sir? My cape and belt say otherwise, wouldn't you agree? And as soon as I'm released from this impenetrable prison, I'll just have to prove it to you."

Noah snickered at the dramatic bear and then took a peek through the bars. He noticed that the steel poles were quite a distance apart.

"Hold on…can't you just squeeze through the bars if you wanted out so badly?"

Koda grabbed his belly, pushing it in as much as he could. "Unfortunately, it appears that my last meal may have been a tad more than I should've eaten. Sometimes,

I just can't help myself. Yesterday, I got stuck and the guards had to douse me with butter to free me. It was a sticky situation, but delicious nonetheless. They treat people quite well in here, despite us being prisoners."

Noah agreed, and that brought him a sense of comfort. Not for himself, but for Lucia.

"So, Sir Noah, if you aren't in here for the untimely demise of your own Angel, then what brings you to a place such as this?"

"Everyone probably says this, but I'm not really sure, honestly. We'd just arrived in Stone Cutter, and the next thing I knew I was laying on the ground with handcuffs on. They were calling my Angel, 'the Angel of Death,' but I don't know what they meant by that."

Koda's eyes grew wide and his mouth flew open. "Hold on a second—are you telling me that you're united with the Angel of Death? Now you're yanking my tail. Every adventurer knows that the Angel of Death was lost to time hundreds of years ago"

"So you actually know what they're talking about?" Noah took a seat on the bed across from Koda, and his shoulders slumped as he pondered. *Lucia...the Angel of Death...* He looked up at Koda again. "What do you know about the Angel of Death?"

Suddenly, Koda's voice became much more serious. "History doesn't paint her kindly, that's for sure. It's actually somewhat of a story lost to time thanks to the damage caused. But have you heard of the Angel Wars?"

"The Angel Wars...I know a little bit about them, but not much. Just what my grandpa told me when I was younger. From what I understand, it was known as the great war between Engvall and the Kingdom of Solace. The two battled it out over ether resources, I believe."

"Resources, land, power. War is rarely about one thing, if you ask Koda. But regardless, since Angels were a new phenomenon, everyone was trying to harness their powers, and I dare say that if what the people here think is true, then your Angel is the deadliest of them all. Legend says that her powers could slice a region in two. That said, she was meant to have been defeated by a great hero and their Angel to end the war."

Noah balked. *There's no way that could be Lucia. That's not the kind of Angel she is. There has to be more to this story.*

"But don't worry about it, Sir Noah," Koda continued. "I'm sure it's just mistaken identity. I mean really, if there was word of the Angel of Death being back, surely I would've heard it on my many, illustrious travels."

Noah thought for a second, remembering that Lucia had only been awake for a day or so. It was surprising for Stone Cutter to realize that she was awake, but there was no way word could've spread to those in a jail cell so quickly.

"Okay, so you know why I'm in this place. Now you have to share your story. How did you end up in a jail cell?"

Koda tapped his chin. "Well, I was saving this for my tell-all book, but I guess you did share your tale of woe with me first. Fine, I'll spin you a vision of my gripping story, but I must warn you, it is quite tragic, and my cape is not to be used as tissues."

Noah had to admit that the melodramatics of the Ursula were starting to grow on him. He found them endearing, and somehow he was sure that the story wouldn't be a difficult one to hear.

Noah laughed. "Don't worry, I think I can handle it."

"A stone wall of emotion I see. Well, my friend, as one who hails from the great land of the Ursulas, I have traveled a great distance. Though the frigid snow, the pelting rain, the vast sands, and even enduring the scorching heat—all while facing incredible monsters, the likes of which few have stood against. The days were long, the battles mighty, but as the great Ursula—Koda the Adventurer—I stood mighty and tall in the face of danger. After many moons of travel across these great lands, I finally reached this little town known as Stone Cutter. However, when I did, I found myself parched of food and water. My supplies were bone dry. What's an Ursula to do? As I walked, using the remaining willpower I had in my little paws to keep carrying onward, I caught wind of a truly delectable smell. It was intoxicating, a smell so rich in flavour it could make an Ursula faint. So I followed my peckish nose and soon spotted a group of merchant stands. There was food laid out all across these stands, a gift from the Guardian Angel, left for parched adventurers like myself to feast on. Little did I know that in these lands food is not free, and in fact costs something called gold coins. So after being whisked away with a full stomach, I was thrown into these dungeons, forced to await my fated trial. Truly a dark tale indeed."

Noah absorbed the information, astonished. There was an innocence, if not an outright ignorance, in Koda's voice. The Ursula was serious, at least regarding his reason for being in jail. But the added bravado of a seasoned storyteller made it all the more comical.

His story also helped confirmed Noah's assumptions

about Koda. This Ursula was no criminal—at least not the kind that anyone would consider a threat to society. He was the same as Noah, thrown behind bars over a simple misunderstanding.

That said, there was an easy solution that could deal with Koda's problem, and one Noah knew he could handle quickly enough. He reached into the lining of his shorts and pulled out a small burlap sack. It had just a light jingle to it, but he was sure what was inside would be enough to cover the costs. Despite the guards taking his sword when he was detained, they hadn't bothered to search him for anything else, yet another sign that they didn't view him as much of a criminal.

He couldn't help but take a small poke at the bear. "You'd think that for a renowned adventurer such as yourself you'd have heard about the currency in Alterra."

"Yes, well...I guess perhaps it slipped through the cracks..." Koda sheepishly scratched the back of his head.

"Anyway, how much do you owe for...let's call it your adventures?"

"I believe the guards said my tab was 25 of your golden coins."

"25?!" Noah choked out. "That's like a week's worth of food! How could you possibly run up that much of a tab? I mean look at you—your stomach is barely the size of my head!"

Koda rubbed the pale spot on his stomach and said, "Adventuring as extravagantly as I do takes a big appetite, you know."

Noah shook his head, but couldn't help but smile. He dumped some of the bag into his palm and started counting the coins. Each piece of gold had a different shape and number on them. First were the triangular gold coins—those were the ones that Noah had the most of. There were the numbers one, five, ten, twenty-five, and fifty on them. Next were the square gold coins, all with a matching number set. Last were the circular gold coins. Those were less plentiful, but Noah plucked a 10-piece coin, and three 5s before handing them to Koda.

"This should cover your tab. Next time you see the guards, tell them you have the money and to let you out."

Koda took the coins like he'd just been given a mysterious treasure. He felt the outside grooves of the coins along his paw, admiring the shine of the numbers. On the opposite side of the numbers were wings of an Angel. "So this is what you Humans call coins. Fascinating. They're heavier than I expected." He lifted his paw up, and the weight of the coins sank it back down. "I need to make note of this amazing discovery." He grabbed the tiny journal from his hip pocket and started to scribble down words as fast as he could. Once he finished, he reattached it to his belt and looked back up at Noah. "But why are you giving this to me, Sir Noah? Don't you need these coins as well?"

Noah grinned. "It's okay, I have a bit more saved up. Enough to buy food and a night or two at the inn, just as soon as I get out of here. Consider it a gift amongst friends."

"*Friends…*" Koda whispered, beaming. He held the gold in both paws, still admiring it before placing the coins in his sash. "Thank you, Sir Noah!"

There was a brief silence as Noah took a seat on his cot,

realizing that the guards likely wouldn't be coming back for a while. Until then, there wasn't much he could do.

Across from him, Koda let his stubby legs dangle off his cot. "Hey, Sir Noah?"

Noah glanced up. "You don't have to be so formal, you know. Just call me Noah."

"Oh, all right. Well, Noah? Do you mind if I ask you a question? You know…as one who's united?"

Noah sat up. "Uh, yeah, sure. But be warned that I'm quite new to the whole united and Angels thing. I can't say I know much."

"That's all right, I'm sure you'll be able to answer this one. What's it like? To be united and share powers with your Angel?"

Noah thought about the question. It wasn't something he'd given much thought to before now. Everything had happened so fast; there hadn't been much time to consider how it all felt. But there was one word that repeatedly came to mind.

"Safe," he said softly. "It's like your minds become one, and though you're still acting independently, it's as if you can sense what the other is going to do and you can react off it. But it's more than that. When you're connected, there's a warmth that fills your body. It's a really special feeling."

Even as Noah told of his experience, he couldn't help but wonder if it was the same for everyone else. When Bower and Crimson united, did they feel that same warmth and care for each other? If they did, they certainly didn't show it.

Koda took out his notebook again, writing and speaking at the same time. "Interesting, very interesting. I've *always* wanted to unite, Sir Noah. The concept of Angels and mortals being able to combine their mind and spirit to channel their strengths has long been a fascination of mine. But sadly, even as great of an adventurer as I am, I have yet to find my own Angel. It just hasn't been in the cards so far, but an Ursula can still dream."

A memory flashed in Noah's mind. It was his first real introduction to Angels back when he was entering Engvall. The Angel ceremony, when four Engvall citizens were presented with soul stones and attempting to unite. Two managed to summon their own Angels, but two failed.

"Right. Not everyone can ascend."

Koda continued, "They say that it takes a strong heart and a resolute mind to be graced with the presence of an Angel. Obviously, there's no doubt I have been burdened with both these attributes, but you also need to get your hands on a soul stone. Tricky things to get hold of, they are. My understanding is that in the central region of Drake, more specifically in the city of Solace, they have an Angel registry, where one may apply for a soul stone. Contrary to that, the city of Engvall in Ekholm will sometimes hand you a soul stone if you reach a high enough rank in their army. Those two areas are said to be in control of nearly all the soul stones in Alterra, and all other places across the land must register new soul stones with them. After that, Sir Noah, they'll be the ones to first judge if you're fit to wield the power of an Angel."

"Is that where you're heading? To Drake or Ekholm to get your own Angel?"

Koda shook his head. "I dare say that is not a wise idea. After the great war took place, Ursulas and those two cities did not quite see eye to eye on matters. Those tensions are why we decided to move into seclusion. This adventurer knows when it's wise to stay away from certain places. Unfortunately, this means that for me to find a soul stone, I'll have to come up with some other way."

"Oh…well, did you have a plan? Is that why you came here?"

"Again, I'm afraid not. Soul stones are quite rare to come across. If they're not granted to you by the Emperor of Engvall or the Prince of Solace, then you'll be hard-pressed to find one in the wild. The other way is to have it passed down through families. Angels turn to spirits when their united dies, and their soul stones lose strength for a period of time, and so they're kept within the families as protectors, but because of the Ursula seclusion this is of course not an option." Koda hopped off the bed and suddenly seemed skeptical. He marched back and forth like a detective hot on the case. "But now that I think about it, since you did not know these facts, my keen intuition tells me that none of those paths apply to you, my good sir. No, you happened across your Angel in a different way, a far more unconventional way." Koda tapped the rounded fur on his chin. "I suppose there *is* one other way that comes to mind for people to get their hands on a soul stone…that is to say by killing the united and taking the stone by force…" Koda's curious face was fixated on Noah's.

But before he could continue his investigation, Noah adamantly shut him down.

"I didn't kill anyone for my soul stone! I would never do such a thing!"

Koda dropped his innocent third degree and spun

around waving his paw. "Indeed, you're right. And plus, Sir Noah, you don't look like the type that would hold up in a fight anyway."

Noah readied to fire back but decided to keep his mouth shut.

Before the conversation went any further, the two felt an intense rumbling from overhead. Dirt began spraying down from the ceiling and Koda lost his balance. As the rumbling intensified, so too did the stirring of others in their cells.

"What's happening?!?" Koda cried, his voice muffled and shaky amidst the tremors.

The extreme vibrations stopped, and Noah and Koda both got to their feet. "I don't know, but I can't imagine it's good."

That's when the reality of what might be taking place above them started to invade Noah's mind. *Please tell me this isn't Lucia's doing, The Angel of Death. No, they're wrong! She wouldn't do this.* But he could pinpoint one suspect who might. *What if the Engvall army learned that we were in Stone Cutter and came for Lucia?*

Noah lunged for the steel bars of the cell, gripping them with all his might. There was no chance he'd break free, he knew that. But even so, he was desperate to try.

Suddenly, he felt a sinking feeling in his chest and his heart began to ache. He took a deep breath and closed his eyes, remembering his grandfather's training. Calm and focused wins the battle.

"Sir Noah, what are you doing?" Koda asked.

Noah spun around, doing his best to heed his grandpa's words. "We need to find a way out of here. I think Stone Cutter could be in danger."

"I see!" Koda exclaimed, whipping his cape around and grinning fiercely. "Leave this to me—I'll break us free! I am Koda the Adventurer, after all. I cannot simply stand by if there's danger afoot!"

The diminutive Ursula lowered his shoulder, and like a cannonball flung himself forward as fast as his little legs could carry him. With a powerful battle cry, he smashed into the steel bars. But, predictably, he smacked into them and came to a dead stop before collapsing backward. There wasn't so much as a dent in the bars.

He tried to get to his feet, dizzy and disoriented. When he looked up, he could've sworn that he was seeing four of Noah dancing around the room. "It would appear that those bars are quite indestructible." he lamented, shaking the stars out of his head.

But just as they were feeling helpless, two guards and an elegant Angel came rushing through the cell halls. The group bypassed all the other cells and headed straight for Noah. In a hurry, they unlocked the cell and flung the door open. Out from behind the guards, the Angel of the group stepped forward.

"You are Noah, yes?" she asked politely and yet panic-stricken.

"Yes, what's going on?"

"My name is Ophelia. I am Angel to Elder Adidas, and we have commissioned your release in order to help the Arch Angel Lucia fight off our invaders. You are hereby released."

"Invaders? This must be Engvall's doing!"

"It is not. Though we have not confirmed anything, it looks like a group of rogue Angels. That said, we can deal with the aftermath later. We must hurry."

"Right. Come on, Koda—we gotta go!"

Koda didn't need to be told twice, shaking off his daze and making a break for the exit. But when he got to the doorway, he was instead met with a sword scraping the ground. He stopped as the tip of the blade touched his nose. "My, that's a mighty big sword…" Koda said, his eyes following the blade toward the guard, who locked his no-nonsense eyes with him.

"You're not going anywhere, fur ball," the guard threatened. Koda swallowed hard, cautiously taking hold of the sword's tip and placing it on the stone ground beside him. "I see."

"He's with me! He'll help fight the invaders!"

"What?" both Koda and the guard gawked in unison, but Ophelia didn't have time for negotiations.

"Fine, take the Ursula—we don't have time for debates. Make way for the town center. Lucia is heading there as we speak."

Noah grabbed his new friend by the paw, hoisting him into the air and onto his shoulder. "Hold on, Koda…we're about to put those adventuring skills of yours to the test!"

Koda grabbed onto Noah's collar, hanging on like a bag flapping in the wind as Noah rushed down the hall to help his Angel.

"But why would Angels be invading a place like this? I fancy that quite peculiar," Koda wondered.

"Don't know, but we need to find Lucia, and quick."

Even if it wasn't Engvall and the Emperor coming after Lucia, he was confident that their threat was related to her.

The unlikely duo turned the corner, running through the barracks of the cells where there were no soldiers around.

Most of the barracks were empty as well; walls bare of swords, axes, katanas, and bows—all taken for battle.

From the corner of his eye, Koda noticed a sparkle. "Wait!" he yelled, forcing Noah to a skidding halt.

"Wait!? For what? We don't have time for waiting!"

Koda hopped off Noah's shoulder and rushed over to a crate filled to the brim with various objects. Some looked like jewelry and others were various swords, though the quality appeared shabby at best.

Growing impatient, Noah finally yelled, "There's no time for this!"

"Hold your horses, I just know they stuck it in here somewhere." Koda drawled, tossing all the perceived junk out from the boxes. Throughout all the clanking and tumbling of items being tossed aside, Koda finally pulled out the object of his desire. "Got it!" he cheered. In his paws he held up a short, golden wand, at the top of which was a circular shape with a jewel floating in the middle. He strapped the wand to his back and started rushing over to Noah before saying, "Where's your sword, Sir Noah? You can't possibly go into a fight without a weapon!"

Noah reached around his back and realized that Koda was right. For a moment he'd forgotten that he'd been stripped of his weapon upon arrest. "Uh…right." His eyes began scanning the room. Unlike Koda's wand, which could easily fit in a box, Oathkeeper was far bigger and much harder to miss, but it was nowhere to be seen. *It's not here! Wait…what if…*

He remembered Lucia summoning her sword with just a simple thought. It was an ability only an Angel had, and one he couldn't hope to replicate. But then it dawned on him: if Lucia was already in the fight, she would've needed to summon Oathkeeper.

Now who's the one wasting time?" Koda said, pulling Noah from his thoughts.

"Right." Noah said, grabbing the sword closest to him. It was much less glamorous than Oathkeeper and lacked the same grit and strength that his grandfather's sword once did, but it was the best option available. "Come on, we need to go!"

Noah threw the scarab around his back and scooped Koda up before hurrying outside.

Unlike on the way in, the gates of passage were left open, and outside there were no guards in sight. Noah figured they must've all headed into town to help out.

Once outside, it took the two a few moments to gauge their whereabouts, but then a giant shadow drew their attention overhead.

"Whoa, what is that?!" Noah gawked, staring up at the object blotting out the sun.

"It's…it's an airship!" Koda marvelled. It was passing over the town, and they could see some green flakes rising to the base of the airship.

"Something tells me we should probably follow that…" Noah said.

"Right, Sir Noah!"

They took off down the dirt path, both holding their breath in fear of what was to come.

CHAPTER 10
POWERS UNITED

The sky was a mix of strange green ash and smoke floating in the air. Because the jail was located outside of Stone Cutter's general town, Koda and Noah needed to hurry.

Just hold on a little longer, Lucia. I'm on my way, I promise.

Following the path back, Noah and Koda continued staring up at the monstrous airship. The sounds of its rutters made thinking difficult, but at least they were both searching for the same signs on the ship. Upon the side of the ship were strange letters that Noah couldn't read. But he knew of a great adventurer who might.

"Hey, Koda, can you read those symbols?"

"Well, it's hard to say for sure, but I think it says…Monster of the Seraph Sea? Or at least that's how it translates in *my* language. In English, I think it means…Leviathan."

"Leviathan?"

"It seems like that could be the cause of our problems, Sir Noah."

"Right. Let's hurry," Noah insisted, picking up his pace.

As they closed in on Stone Cutter's front gate, they noticed a group of guards, five in total. They were holding off what looked like some fairly strange creatures. From afar, they certainly looked like no regular monsters that Noah was used to facing. They were generic looking Angels.

"Wait, are those Angels?" Noah asked. His eyes darted around, trying to figure out where the united mortals with them were, but nobody was around.

"Sir Noah, these aren't ordinary Angels," Koda whispered.

"What do you mean?"

"All Angels are unique creatures and wear a ring similar to their united. And their eyes pop with a special glow. However, just look at these things, Sir Noah. If I didn't have my wits about me, I'd say they're more like clones of Angels."

"Angel clones? That doesn't sound good."

The two came to a stop, observing how the clones fought. They were mindless, locking on to a target and attacking with unbridled conviction. On the bright side, at least they weren't showing any signs of blessings.

"We need to help them," Noah said. He drew his temporary blade and charged into the fray, blocking the attacks of an incoming Angel clone.

One of the guards fell to his backside and stared up as Noah grunted, using the face of his sword to block the Angel's impending slash.

The guard's eyes opened wide. "You…you're with the Angel of Death…"

"We can talk about how wrong you are about Lucia later. Now get up and fight!" Noah gritted his teeth. He thrust the Angel's sword up and slashed horizontally, sending the monster backwards.

"This is bad," one of the guards said, trying to hold off two Angels of his own. "They just keep raining down from the sky…there's no end to them."

The group started to backpedal, hoping to put some space between them and the vicious Angels. As they did, they noticed strange green particles falling from the sky. They were like snowflakes, but once Noah inhaled them, he felt a sudden burn in his lungs.

It's ether, like back in the ruins. He and the guards started coughing, making it much more difficult to fight.

"What the hell is this stuff?! Some sort of poison gas?" one of the guards sputtered

"No, it's ether!" Noah said. He tried to cover his mouth with his sleeve. The particles rained down, and for all the issues they were causing, it was doing wonders for the Angels. Their eyes were beginning to glow blood red, filling them with a fighting fury.

Noah and the guards glanced up at the airship. "We don't have a way of taking that thing down, do we?"

"No, Stone Cutter doesn't carry military weapons like other places. Only the Kerfoot capital has an arsenal," one of the guards pointed out.

"Crap, this isn't good," another guard lamented. "If they're this strong, the rest of the guards in town won't be able to hold them off."

Noah blocked an incoming blunt force strike from a smaller futuristic Angel and its spear. He tensed his muscles, holding it back when he heard another guard cough out, "Help me!"

Noah shoved the Angel back and spun to his left, bearing witness to an awful sight. One of the guards were being held by the neck, the clone Angel gripping his windpipe like it was a squishy toy. His legs were dangling as he flailed in hopes of breaking free.

"We need to help him!" Noah yelled. He bolted away from his own opponent, heading for the save. With the Angel distracted, Noah jumped high in the air, roaring as he thrust his sword with precision and speed. It blew through the Angel's body like butter, even more green ether spewing out from the wound. The guard dropped to the ground in a heap, sucking back oxygen while the Angel collapsed, eventually fading into the particles that floated to the sky.

From behind, one of the guards shouted, "Kid, look out!"

Noah spun around, throwing his sword up to defend, but the Angel charging at him was faster. He squeezed his eyes shut waiting for the impending impalement.

But suddenly, a ball of fire whizzed past his ear, burning the hairs on his neck before exploding into the Angel.

"Sir Koda to the recuse!" the Ursula shouted gallantly, striking a showman's pose with his wand pointed to the sky and his cape flapping in the wind.

Shocked, Noah spun around just in time to see Koda's entire body glowing with a red and yellow aura, while under his feet was a mystical circle that moved like gears in a clock.

"Wait, you can use magic?! But you don't even have ether orbs on you!" Noah gawked.

"I have many talents, Sir Noah—magic just happens to be an Ursula special. Now buckle up, 'cause we're not done here!"

Noah nodded, regaining his composure and rushing forward as the next Angel did the same. With the advantage on his side, Noah sliced through the Angel with ease, dropping it to its knees before it evaporated into particles.

"Phew, that was a close one," Noah panted.

With two of the clones down, the guards were beginning to force the others back. Progressing in this way would allow them to reach town shortly.

Meanwhile, Noah couldn't help but stare at the diminutive bear who'd just saved his life. How did he do it?

"Okay, you have to explain what just happened. I've never seen anyone use magic without ether orbs."

"It's quite simple—I'm just amazing, aren't I, Sir Noah?"

The moment of intrigue caused the battle itself to slip Noah's mind. But when the ground rumbled below their feet again followed by an explosion in the distance, he was pulled right back to reality.

"Fine, but you're explaining how you did that when this is over!" he said, scooping up Koda. "Now let's get going. We're gonna need that magic of yours!"

Smoke continued blanketing the skies of the town square and was becoming thick as Noah approached the gates. He could hear storming feet like herds of bulls trying to escape, which was slowly drown out by constant cries of terror. When he comprehended the reality of the situation, he was struck with a pang of guilt.

Did he at least, in part, bear some culpability for Stone Cutter's current situation? After all, if these Angels were on the hunt for Lucia, then bringing her here was the direct cause. And now they were ransacking homes and wrecking the innocent lives of many, all in mindless acts of violence. He needed to find Lucia and put an end to all this before anyone else was hurt.

Getting through Stone Cutter was tricky. The town was small enough, but having only walked the streets once, Noah struggled to find the shortest path. All he could do was listen and focus on the cries of battle piercing the air, using them as his guide. He soon spotted a glowing light that broke up the smoke. *Lucia?*

Keeping his pace steady, he heard the ominous words, "Is this *really* the best the Arch Angel has? Surely you can do better than this."

Now he knew he was on the right course. Clashes from the battle grew deafeningly loud. He was close. Through the smoke, Noah burst forward, his sword deflecting the blade of an attacker while he cut in front of Lucia.

"Stay away from my Angel!" Noah shouted.

Stunned, Lucia stood behind her mortal, whispering, "You made it." There was an unfamiliar power and urgency in Noah's voice that took her by surprise. No softness, no empathy — just stone-cold determination.

"Well, isn't this an unexpected turn…the unified finally arrives to save the day," Marco laughed, pulling his sword back and retreating from the fray.

"Sir Noah! Above!" Koda pointed to the sky, where the second Angel, Petra, was descending with a hammer directly overhead.

Noah lifted his sword using the flat of his blade to block the incoming blow. The recoil sent Koda soaring backwards, bouncing like a tennis ball off the ground and to a painful stop.

"Koda!" Noah yelled.

"I'm just fine, Sir Noah! Just a little dizzy is all," the Ursula warbled, spinning around in circles until he collapsed.

"If I were you, I'd be focusing on *us*, not the bear," Petra growled. She remained suspended in air as the weight of her hammer cracked the ground below them, forcing Noah into the slowly forming crater. The hammer was inching closer to his face, and he could feel his flimsy weapon, grabbed in haste, starting to crack.

"Noah, duck!!!"

Hearing Lucia's words, Noah did as his Angel demanded and dropped to his chest in the crater. With perfect timing, a crescent-moon-shaped ray of light soared over his head, smacking Petra and tossing her through the air.

Lucia hurried into the crater and helped Noah to his feet. "Took you long enough! Are you okay, at least?"

Noah grinned wearily. "Nothing a nice nap couldn't fix, but we'll have time to sleep later. Who *are* these Angels?"

"They're agents from Alterra, Marco and Petra—and they're tough. Marco can deflect ether, so my halo blade won't work, and Peta's hammer creates spikes along the ground, which means that getting in close isn't ideal, either. My power alone isn't enough to win this. We're gonna need a strategy." Lucia held out her majestic blade and handed it to her partner. "Here—I think this suits you better than that piece of scrap metal."

As Noah grabbed the hilt of Oathkeeper, a jolt of power surged through his arm—that familiar warmth he was becoming accustomed to. A comfort that gave him the courage to fight whatever foe stood in his way.

"Oh, yeah, this is what I'm talking about! Let's show these guys who they're messing with!"

Noah quickly swung the sword around for practice before fixing his stare on Petra and Marco, watching this show without a care in the world.

"So the young hero arrives to save his beloved Angel in her moment of need — a story as old as time. But I dare say that this hero might be in over his head," Marco laughed. The arrogance was brimming off his words, but Noah could see through it. There was power in his voice, which was especially advantageous if he could handle Lucia. As for Petra, he was well aware of her power already.

"Lover boy is right," Petra seethed. "Prepare to die, kid. The Arch Angel is coming with *us*."

It was clear that the agents of Alterra were not afraid of Noah, and they were in no rush to force a fight.

The four stood meters apart, the air growing thick with tension as they waited for Noah to make the first move. Angels and guards were still fighting around the town, but that never crossed their minds. All they cared about was the mission right in front of them.

Noah whispered, "I think I've got a plan. Just cover me," before rushing forward.

Lucia followed his orders and raised her hands to surround Noah with an aura of light. *"You better know what you're doing."*

"Don't worry — we've got this. I'm not letting anyone take you for their own purposes. Your life is yours and yours alone! They have no right to try and control it for themselves!"

As Noah moved, the light coursing through Oathkeeper grew ferocious, and far more intense than what he'd experienced while they were trudging through the jungles toward Stone Cutter.

His first option was to engage Marco head on. Since the Angel was an issue from a distance, that was the only logical choice. He had a hunch with this strategy; he needed to believe that Petra would be hesitant to attack with her spikes, as long as her partner was in the way.

Noah locked swords with Marco, the two of them tiptoeing as sparks blasted with each swing.

"You're gonna regret coming after Lucia!" Noah said through clenched teeth. Even with Lucia's strength infused in him, Marco refused to budge.

"Sorry, prince charming," Marco retorted, "but I can't let you keep the Arch Angel's power all for yourself. It's nothing personal, but this is where you'll meet your end." He leapt back, high into the air and away from Noah.

Lucia froze. *"Noah, look out!"*

Being Noah's second set of eyes, she realized Marco's plan and managed to warn Noah before it could be activated. Petra slammed her hammer on the ground, shaking the stone pathway while spikes shot up, ready to impale Noah.

But because of Lucia's warning, Noah shifted his body and swung the blade as if Lucia was guiding his hands. His swing unleashed a halo blade that sliced through the spikes with ease.

"Thanks!" Noah was relieved.

But Lucia knew that they were far from done. *"Heads up!"*

Marco soared downward from the sky, beginning a series of thrusting motions. He attacked like a trained artist, never leaving an opening for retaliation. Noah was steadfast in his counterstrikes, but the Angel was relentless. It was becoming apparent Noah's skill was outclassed, even with Lucia's assistance.

"You're not bad, hero," Marco taunted, "but the power of the Arch Angel won't help you now. You're in over your head and this is a different game. You should just quit while you're ahead." Marco spun off of Noah's foiled thrust, landing a bone-crushing punch into Noah's ribs. Noah flew backward and collapsed to the ground, his sword thrown into the air. He grabbed at his ribs, wincing.

"Finish him now, Petra!" Marco ordered. Through the darkened sky, Petra sailed overhead and swung her hammer, sending a staggering flurry of spikes toward Noah.

"I've got you!" Flying out in front, Lucia thrust her arms forward, forcing a barrier around both of them. The spikes smashed into the impenetrable defenses and held up with ease.

Noah got to one knee, breathless from the shock. "Thanks, Lucia…that was a close one."

"Can you still fight?"

"Yeah, I'm fine. But these two are tough. I can't touch them!"

"I have a new idea. I need a little bit of time, but I think we can win this with one shot!"

Then Noah heard the weak patter of footsteps from behind.

"Once again, Koda the Adventurer has come to the rescue! Stand back, my fair Angel…I shall handle these two!"

Lucia glanced at the Ursula, confused. She raised an eyebrow and said, "Noah, who is this?"

"Don't worry I trust him. After all, he's a great adventurer."

Lucia shook her head but said, "Fine, I don't care if he's fader or not, we just need time."

Despite Lucia's utter confusion about this flamboyant addition to their team, out from the barrier Koda stepped, wand in hand and cape flapping in the wind. He puffed out his chest, marching forward with dramatic bravado.

Marco balked. "That's your trump card? A walking bear cub?" He held his sword parallel to the ground, ready to end Koda in one blow.

But Petra saw something else, noticing the elegance of the golden wand in the bear's paw. "Hold it, Marco—that's an Ursula! Brace yourself!"

"Ursulas don't exist anymore!" Marco retorted.

"Oh, I can assure you, my Angel friends—I am very real and my unparalleled magic knows no bounds." Koda twirled his wand, drawling lines in the air like an artist. It was a mystical display—an artform, even. With each movement, various circles formed under Koda's feet, just like Noah had briefly seen previously.

"That bear isn't normal," Lucia whispered, rapt at the enchanting display.

Koda snapped his wand forward, and out from the front facing spell circle shot three meteors like fireballs. They hurled at Marco and Petra rapidly, leaving a trail of smoke behind.

Now that Koda was holding up his end of the plan, Lucia returned her focus to Noah and their shared Oathkeeper. They both had a hand on the hilt, one over the other, as it began to exude its awesome power. Lucia was channeling everything she could, but this time, so was Noah. It was a surreal feeling for him; it felt like the life was being sucked straight from his body. His face went pale and his head became dizzy, but he refused to let go. He understood what was happening. The ether in his body was being converted thanks to Lucia and was charging their sword. Since his body lacked even a fraction of the ether that Angels had, the effects on him carried more of a punch. But he could handle it.

As for the impending fireballs, Marco smirked and raised his long katana in front of him. "Did you already forget? Your magic still contains ether. It's of no use against my blessing."

Faint pulsations formed in the air, like small ripples. The meteors got close, but once they were caught in the effects of Marco's ether field they plummeted into the ground, causing a fiery explosion of smoke and debris.

Through the smoke, they heard Marco's voice again. "I'll give you credit, Ursula—that level of magic is quite impressive. But it's a pity that that's all you've got."

Petra gripped her hammer tight. "Now how about we see how much resistance that fur puts up against spikes?" She raised her hammer, ready to slam it down, while Koda took a step back, terrified.

"Uh, Sir Noah? Ms. Lucia? Feel free to step in any time now!"

"Not yet—we need more time!" Lucia yelled back.

There was a sinister glint in Petra's eyes as her hammer came crashing down. Spikes began jetting up, overlapping on top of one another as they raced for Koda.

Koda's face turned to complete horror before he

whipped his wand forward and yelled, "Dome of Protection!"

Like Lucia's own blessing, a dome formed around Koda. Though far smaller in scale, it proved just as powerful. The spikes crashed into its barrier erupting in smoke that flooded the battlefield.

"Koda!" Noah cried out, not sure if his new friend had managed to protect himself in time.

"Noah, he's fine! You need to focus!" Lucia ordered. She knew that full concentration would be their only chance to achieve maximum strength.

Noah nodded, the grip on their sword becoming tighter. He felt a jolt run through his body, and an overwhelming flood of power took hold. He shared a knowing look with Lucia, who nodded in response, "We're ready. Just follow my lead, and let my power flow through you! We'll end this in one shot!"

"All right, let's do this!"

The smoke was beginning to fade but it was just enough for them to get the drop on their opponent. Rays of light repelled the smoke, and Lucia and Noah soared through the air. Everyone stuck on the ground glanced up, including Koda in awestruck amazement, and even Petra and Marco appeared highly concerned.

The air stilled as though time was slowing down. Noah could see everything happening in half-speed, or maybe even slower. Or was he just moving incredibly fast? He couldn't tell, but he did know that his body temperature was rising quickly. A burning heat nestled in his chest that made him feel incredible. He was sure it was Lucia's power combining with his. Together, as they held Oathkeeper, they were one in mind and body.

Moving in perfect sync, they thrust their sword down, unleashing their full power.

"Halo slash!"

They pummelled the sword downward, colliding with Marco's katana and Petra's hammer. Shockwaves cut through the air, slicing light poles and billboards in the town's center. But both the Alterra agents were still not defeated. They continued to resist the attack, though struggling more than previously.

Petra was incensed. "You're really starting to get on my nerves, kid! You can't even use the Arch Angel's powers right!" Holding her own just fine she swung back, and in a split-second reaction, Lucia grabbed Noah by the waist and flew backwards, skidding next to Koda.

"This is just more proof that some stupid kid isn't fit to wield the Arch Angel's power!" Marco yelled, dashing forward and choosing to go on the offensive. He pressed Lucia, both of them moving with skill and grace as they deflected each other's advances.

Petra joined in the attack, but Lucia swiftly dodged her blitzes with masterful acrobatics, flipping backward as spikes rose from the ground.

"Damn, I really thought that would work!" Noah sweated.

Beside him, Koda put his paw on his friend's leg. "It was a valiant effort, Sir Noah. These two are indeed worthy opponents."

"There's no way Lucia can take them both! Can't you use some of that magic of yours to help her?"

Koda shook his head. "I'm afraid not, Sir Noah. Even

my magic is limited by my life force, and I used up most of it on that meteor spell. Any more would be much too risky."

Noah attempted to get to his feet, though his body was ragged. Using Lucia's power in such a way was now having ill effects — something that Marco picked up on.

"Petra, the boy!" he ordered.

Petra instantly changed course and began smacking her spikes like they were golf balls, sending them firing at Noah and Koda.

Noah closed his eyes, throwing his arms up to brace for impact, while Koda was so petrified that he grabbed his ears and folded them in front of his eyes. Luckily, before the attack could land, Lucia appeared in front of him, blocking with her barrier.

Noah glanced up and got to one knee. "Thanks, Lucia."

"You're welcome, but get up — we're not done yet!"

"Right! We can't give in yet. Gramps would never accept that!" Noah pushed himself upright, taking the sword from Lucia. As he did, the light symbolizing their unity tethered itself to him again. His aches and pains subsided and he narrowed his focus. "Cover me!"

Noah charged forward with a full arsenal of steam. Lucia once again raised her hands, thus supercharging Noah.

Noah locked horns with Marco, whose smug arrogance was written all over his face for the entire battle. He was treating their fight like one big game — one he was sure he would win.

"Why are you doing this, kid? Are you just trying to be her knight in shining armour? Do you even know who you're trying to protect? Are you aware of the power that remains locked away in that Angel? It's more than your mind could possibly fathom, and it's a power that's best served with us."

Noah gritted his teeth, fighting to keep his composure. "I don't care about whatever power Lucia has. She's my friend and I made a promise to her! The last thing I'll do is let you take her somewhere she doesn't want to go!"

Lucia felt a new blessing in her heart. Hearing those words, she knew that in the short time since being awakened, Noah was the only one who continued to believe in her, the only one who refused to condemn her. It made her feel loved — vastly unlike the people of Stone Cutter, the Engvall army, or even history. It warmed her soul in ways she didn't know possible. And as it did, the power she kept transferring to Noah grew stronger.

Oathkeeper's light began to expand, flickering like violent flames. *So she was holding back. I guess I shouldn't be surprised after she'd been asleep for all those years*, Marco thought, knowing that he was losing ground. He leapt back, narrowly missing a slash from Noah.

A still settled over the battlefield. Finally, Petra and Marco were showing a bit of wear and tear for their efforts. But Noah was also quite fatigued. He found it hard to stand straight, his chest rising and falling as he felt the burn in his lungs. His legs were beginning to shake, and the effort to hold up his sword was a clear struggle.

Marco ran his hand through his hair, turning his nose up at Noah. "Guess you're a little better than I thought. Even so, looks like the Arch Angel's power is beginning to wear you down. If you keep it up, you'll be dead in minutes."

"He's right, Noah—we can't keep this up." Lucia said. She was beginning to roll back her power, trying to temper Noah's pain.

"Well, this is quite the precarious position we find ourselves in," Koda added.

"No, I'm fine." Noah said through panting breath. "We give up now and they're gonna take Lucia away. I'm not letting them do that—not until she's got her memories back."

"Bold statement, kid," Marco interjected. "You've got guts, but that'll only carry you so far." He arched his sword as the fire around him turned his blade a fiery red. His sword scraped the ground, ready to strike Noah down, when he suddenly heard a stampede behind him. From all four corners came a storm of guards, all with their Angels. Perhaps they were no match for the clones alone, but they were overwhelming in these numbers.

"Damn, it looks like the cavalry finally arrived," Petra moaned.

Marco glanced up to the sky where Leviathan was overhead, then smirked and lowered his sword. "It's fine. I think we've gathered all the information we need." He turned to face Lucia before taking a bow. "My dear Arch Angel, it has been a pleasure for you to grace us with your presence once more. Until we meet again." He raised his sword to the sky and a beam of light shot down from Leviathan. It swallowed up Marco and Petra, vanishing with a flicker before everyone's eyes.

Everyone finally let out a sigh of relief, but with the battle over and the adrenaline of their fight quickly leaving Noah's body, he started to wobble. He jammed the sword in the dirt, using it as a crutch to hold himself up. His hair fell down in front of his eyes.

Lucia walked up behind him and went to grab his arm, but Noah fell forward before she could, collapsing into her arms.

"Sir Noah!" Koda called, hurrying to his aid. But he came to a sudden stop when he heard a strange noise, like a faint whisper. "Is he…snoring?"

Lucia glanced down at her partner, then up at Koda, a faint smile on her lips. "Noah really is a strange one. Come on—let's find him a bed."

CHAPTER 11
IN THIS TOGETHER

After the battle against Petra, Marco, and the cloned Angels they'd unleashed, Stone Cutter had suffered its fair share of damage once again. It was nothing in comparison to the days of old that saw the entire town leveled instantly, but still there was a growing fear. Casualties were kept to a minimum through the guards' hard work, which everyone was grateful for, but most were still unaware of Lucia's involvement in saving them.

They had a few reasons for discounting Lucia's efforts, which she discussed with Elder Adidas afterwards. The first one was simple. They didn't want the reaction it would no doubt attract to stoke the flames of fear. Yes, Lucia had fought on their side and protected them, and that was certainly a good thing, but it was also evident that she was the source of the attack. Had she not stepped foot in Stone Cutter, the town never would've faced the enormous threat that it did. It was hard to guess how public opinion would view this news, and it just felt safer for them to shine the spotlight elsewhere.

That wasn't to say that Adidas or even the guards weren't grateful for the Arch Angel's help. Once the battle was over and now that Noah was completely exhausted, the guards even offered to take him and their small group back to the palace to provide shelter and nourishment.

It was a generous offer, and one made in good faith, but Lucia could still sense some of the tension due to her presence. She was sure that some people would always believe her actions were nothing more than a facade to bring about a false sense of security, a lure for her to strike again.

Fortunately, the Elder did not appear to harbor those same concerns — at least not anymore.

The next morning, Noah awoke and rubbed his blurry eyes, feeling like he'd slept for days. Once he moved his arms, he felt the sting of bruises all over his body. He looked down, realizing that he was enveloped in thick, warm blankets. They were soft and fluffy, not like the gritty, hole-filled blankets at his home. He lay on his back, his body refusing to move as he stared up at the stone architecture of the ceiling. A mosaic of layered stones of different colours shimmered and twinkled, not unlike some of the other places he'd spotted in Stone Cutter.

Yawning loudly, he tried to recall his last memory but struggled. He tried to push himself up but failed at that, too. There was no strength left in his muscles. He sighed, sinking further into the bed.

But before he could return to his restful slumber, the door creaked open.

"Noah…are you awake? I heard someone yawn in here."

It was Lucia. He tried to crank his neck to the left, only to be met with the sting of his injuries. "Ugh…Lucia… what in Alterra happened? I feel like I just went through one of grandpa's boot camps."

Lucia stepped into the room, grabbing a chair from the nearby desk and sitting next to Noah's bed.

"Not quite a boot camp, but you certainly put your body through some heavenly torture, that's for sure. I was beginning to wonder if you were ever going to wake up."

"Really? How long have I been out?"

"Just over two days. But I guess I really shouldn't be surprised. I might not have my memories, but I do know that pumping a mortal full of power through unity is tough on them, especially for someone who isn't accustomed to it. In fact, if not for Ophelia's heal blessing, you'd probably be feeling even worse."

Her words began to jog Noah's memory, and bit by bit he recalled the previous day's events.

"That's right…Marco and Petra…" Noah reached to rip the covers off, but Lucia abruptly stopped him, shaking her head.

"Not so fast there, bucko. I put your body through a lot of stress and it needs the proper time to recover." She sounded almost maternal.

"Oh, so that's what happened…" Noah whispered, recalling the recent events. But he hardly blamed Lucia, instead doing his best to flash his trademark grim and look at his partner. "Well, I guess I'm just gonna need to toughen up then."

"No, that's not what I—"

"It's okay, Lucia. I know what you're thinking, even if we're not united anymore. You did what you felt was needed for us to win. You know, when we first met, I could feel this incredible power inside you. It was magical. But now that I've seen what you're capable of when you're not holding back, it's clear what I have to do. If I'm going to help you get your memories back, it's up to me to learn to harness that power."

"Actually, I wanted to talk to you about that…" Lucia was suddenly reserved, averting her glare from Noah. She grabbed at her arm, her face fretful. "I'm not sure this is a good idea."

"What do you mean? Don't you want to get your memories back?"

Lucia searched for the right words, her fears evident.

Those fears began after speaking to the Elder and learning of the destruction she'd brought on the people of Stone Cutter. Hearing those tales and understanding the pain inflicted was a difficult pill to swallow.

She turned back to look at Noah, his concerned smile and comforting eyes making things a little easier to share.

"Noah…do you know why everyone keeps calling me the Angel of Death?"

He weakly shook his head. "Not really. I know the Angel of Death was an Angel with incredibly destructive power, or at least that's what Koda told me. But nothing else."

"Well, Koda's correct. And though I don't recall the atrocities of that era, the Elder made it clear to me that during the Angel Wars I used my power to wreak havoc on this world. In the Angel Wars, I was a monster… killing Angels and mortals with no remorse—that's how history remembers the Angel of Death. I guess what I'm trying to say is that I'm afraid. Afraid that if I start looking for my memories, I don't know what we might learn about me. And frankly, I'm scared that I can't handle it."

"You're forgetting something. That Angel was full of hate, anger, and, I'd imagine, sadness. But that's not you. The Angel of Death would never put her life on the line to save me. To save the people of Stone Cutter. I don't believe that the Angel of Death would have the ability to show compassion, to care about others, and yet you do. I *know* you do. So I don't believe for a second that you're the Angel of Death, and I never will. If you want a nickname, then you should be called something else…like the Angel of Hope."

"The Angel of Hope?"

"Yeah, because you bring people hope. You fight to protect people. That's who you really are, not some Angel that brings down empires with hatred and rage."

"But…"

Noah spoke softly, keeping his eyes locked with Lucia. "I can't pretend to know what happened in the Angel Wars, or in your past. But what I do know is if you were fighting and caused some sort of damage to Stone Cutter back then…well then I'm sure there must've been no other option. You're a good Angel, Lucia. I can feel it. Not like those two we fought." He placed his hand over his heart. "When we were united, I could feel the goodness in your heart. But I could also feel a sadness tucked deep inside, like a weight was pressing on your chest. And every time someone called you the Angel of Death, it grew heavier. I guess now I understand why."

Lucia was speechless for a moment. She took her time and eventually found the right words. "That's really sweet, Noah. I know it was by accident, but I'm glad it was you that united with me and not somebody else."

A blissful silence filled the room as they both became bathed in happiness and gratitude. For Lucia, there was something powerful in knowing that Noah had her back. It was liberating detaching herself from a name that continued to haunt her. The level of compassion that flowed through his words lifted her spirits and strengthened her faith in reaching her goals.

Finally, Noah sat up in his bed, placing his feet on the cold, stone flooring.

"Hey, what're you doing? You need to rest," Lucia argued.

Noah grinned. "It's all good. I'm fine. Besides, I want to see Koda. I've got some questions for him about that wand he's carrying around."

"Noah, only *you* could be thrown into a jail cell and end up making friends," Lucia smirked.

"Wait, how did you know that?" Noah asked.

"You've been asleep for two days, and our dear Koda the Adventurer loves to tell a good story." Lucia sighed and shook her head. "That bear doesn't shut up."

Noah laughed. "I like him, too."

After helping Noah get out of bed, she guided him down the hall and into a large room on the left side of the stone hall.

Before even opening the doors, the smell of a great feast filled the air. Seasoned meat cooked to perfection, fresh fish seared to delight, and the sweet nectar of local Stone Cutter fruit. Since they were so close to the water, much of the area's food came from fishing, which was just fine by Noah's standards.

Once Noah caught a whiff, he began salivating, and his stomach let out a demanding grumble. He grabbed at his gut before feeling the glare of an incredulous Lucia burning into the back of his neck. He turned around with a sheepish smile. "What, I haven't had a real meal in two days, and I'm hungry."

Lucia sighed. "I guess you're mortal after all. You *do* need to eat."

"Wait, does that mean that Angels *don't* have to eat?"

Lucia shook her head. "We still need food to maintain energy, just not as often. If I really needed to, I could probably stand a week without food just fine."

"Yes, Ms. Lucia is right—we as Angels sustain our energy through the ether produced in our bodies. We mostly eat simply for the purpose of delight. The amount of energy it provides us is little to negligible."

The two looked up to see Ophelia walking toward them. She took a bow and said, "It is nice to properly meet you, Noah. Ms. Lucia has spoken quite highly of you, as has your Ursula friend."

"Noah, this is Ophelia, the Elder's Angel. She's also the one who healed you after fighting Marco and Petra." Lucia then turned to Ophelia. "Thank you again for that, by the way. Your blessing is really amazing."

"Yeah, thanks for that," Noah interjected. "I feel great! Oh, and thanks for letting me use your bed, too. I was beyond tired."

"Of course, it is the least I could do, especially after all you did for our town. My blessing has a number of great recovering abilities, but it also makes the person I heal fall into a deep sleep. Two days is actually quite short, all things considered. However, that is enough about me. You were about to dine, but I just came to inform you that Elder Adidas would like both of you to visit him in his office at your earliest convenience."

"We'll be there soon," Lucia said.

Ophelia left and Noah finally cracked open the doors to the dining hall, again breathing in the delectable aromas. He grinned and said, "It's time to eat!"

But when he stared at the elongated table in front of him, it was little more than just empty with small bits of food. But he was doubly shocked to see the diminutive Ursula, cape strapped around his neck and utility belt latched and snug, sitting on a highchair with a knife and fork in his hands. He was licking his face, then leaned back letting out a boisterous burp.

"Koda?" the two gasped.

"Ah, Sir Noah, you have awoken from your slumber! Boy am I glad. I was becoming worried that our adventuring days together might've been over, and we just can't have that!"

Lucia walked beside the dining table, examining the dozen or so empty plates stacked around Koda. She leaned into the bear and said, "Did you eat all this?" She looked to his stomach. "How in Alterra does an Ursula pack away that much food?"

"My kind has many talents, Ms. Lucia. However, I am not so careless as to leave my adventuring companions with nothing." Koda gestured to the last plate of food on the table. It was a meager piece of fish with a small helping of greens on the side.

"How nice of you," Lucia said, rolling her eyes. She turned to Noah and pointed over to the meager scraps. "It's all yours."

"You sure?"

"Like I said, Angels don't really need food."

Granted the green light, Noah joined Koda in the feast, packing his stomach with as much as he could eat. Luckily, Koda had only eaten the first round, but the Elder's cooks brought plenty more food until the two felt as though they were keeling over.

After their fine meals settled, the three made their way down the hall and entered the Elder's chambers in the back of Stone Cutter's palace. Koda and Noah were in awe of the distinct structures and creativity of the wall art. Lucia, having already been there, lead the way with more urgency. She wanted to hear what the Elder had to say.

When they entered the room, the Elder sat at his desk looking over some papers. Noticing his guests, he stood up, his robes draping along the ground. He bowed and said, "Thank you for coming, Arch Angel." He stepped around his desk and then bowed again. "And to you Noah, and you Koda, as well. We are forever in your debt."

"Of course—we were happy to help," Noah replied.

"I would also like to apologize for having the guards place you in our jails. It was a mistake made in haste, but I hope you can understand. I was simply doing what I felt was necessary to keep Stone Cutter safe."

Noah shrugged it off and said, "It's easily forgivable—

not a worry in the slightest. Besides, I got to meet Koda in there. Without him, I never would've made it to Lucia in the first place."

"All in a day's work for Koda the Adventurer!" the Ursula chimed in.

"Yes, we are grateful to all three of you." Then, staring directly at Lucia, "And I am glad that my misjudgment of you did not prove fatal. Thank you, Arch Angel."

"It was my pleasure, Sir," Lucia said. It was her nature to play it cool, but there was a significant burden lifted from her shoulders as she heard those words, and she was grateful to the Elder.

"All that being said," the Elder continued, "I am afraid we are due for rough times ahead. There is still the matter of our invaders—the agents of Alterra."

"Yeah, I do have a few questions about that," Lucia said. "Obviously, they've restored the once great airship known as Leviathan, but they also mentioned a name…Oberon. When they said that, it jogged my memory but only for a second. Do you know anything about this Oberon, or those Angel clones?"

The Elder shook his head. "I am afraid I do not. All I know about Leviathan is it was a magnificent airship that was sunk in the Angel Wars. As for the name Oberon, that extends past my knowledge—as do those 'Angel clones,' as you call them. I do know this, though. Those two Angels and their army of clones *will* return. Your power is something to behold, but that will make you an enticing treat for many. You must be cautious with your next move."

Lucia looked to Noah and said, "I think we need to get

some information about this Oberon and find out what he wants with me."

"Do you think this is all related to your memories?" Noah asked.

"I do." Lucia then turned to the Elder. "Sir, I know as part of our agreement, I promised to leave Stone Cutter. And seeing the threats that will follow me, I believe even more for that to be a necessity. But would you be able to point us in the right direction or to someone who might have more knowledge about these things?"

The Elder folded his arms in thought, tilted his head, and then smiled, knowingly. "Yes, I believe I can."

He led the group over to his window overlooking the town below and said, "Across the Seraph Sea is a place known as Twin Peaks—a land filled with much beauty and mostly untainted by the technology provided by ether. An old friend by the name of Marleen lives there. She carries with her decades of experience and a wealth of knowledge about the history of Alterra. I have no doubt she will be more than capable of helping you learn of this Oberon. She may even be able to help solve some mysteries surrounding your memories."

"Twin Peaks?" Koda pulled out a map from his sash and rolled it open. "That's all the way on east side of the Drake region! I don't suppose anyone has a boat handy, do they?"

The elder laughed. "I can take care of those arrangements for you—our ports did not suffer too much damage in the attacks and, to my understanding, boats are still free to come and go as they please between the Kerfoot and Drake regions. I will arrange a boat for the three of you to leave in the morning."

"Wow! Thank you—that's great news!" Noah beamed.

"Think nothing of it my boy. However, before you leave, I would like to ask one question of you."

"Sure, what is it?"

"What is it you that seek? The power of the Arch Angel is no small feat to wield, and that is not to ignore the dangers it shall present. It is my understanding that you were wrapped up in this by chance, so I would like to know why a boy such as yourself has chosen to continue this path with the Arch Angel? What is it that bonds you two?"

Noah looked over to Lucia. Every time he stared into her sapphire eyes, he could see the burden within her. He could feel the pain she harboured—a hurt that he could not in good conscious ignore. "I made a promise," he said. "Maybe I wasn't supposed to be the one to reawaken Lucia, but that doesn't matter now. I promised that no matter what it took, I would help her find her memories, to show her that she isn't the Angel of Death everyone thinks she is. She's the Angel of Hope, the one who'll bring hope to all of Alterra. I know that she can. I guess that's what I seek."

"I see." The Elder glanced at Lucia and noticed her quiet softness. "You are a special boy, Noah—I can be certain of that. Remember to trust in each other and keep those bonds strong. Do that, and you might just remain true to your promise."

CHAPTER 12
THE OTHER SIDE

"Well, that was underwhelming," Petra bemoaned. "For the power of being the Arch Angel, that was nothing." Her steps clicked off the metal flooring of Leviathan as she and Marco walked down the vessel's hall.

"You can't really blame her," Marco countered. "She just woke up after being asleep for nearly 300 years. Give her time, and I'm sure she'll return to form."

"She'd better, or she'll be of no use to Oberon."

All around them were metal walls with pulsating green and red lines crossing over each other, looking incredibly futuristic. Though Leviathan was an utterly massive ship, for the most part there wasn't much to it on the inside, at least not anymore. Once a glorious airship that was used to sail the skies while carrying legions of soldiers and their Angels, now it was nothing more than a shell of itself.

There was barely a soul inside. Most of the rooms were

used for storage, though they mostly just contained canisters of ether.

Marco placed his palm on one of the doors in the hall as blue lines raced from his fingertips into small slots on the door. When it slid open, he walked inside, fighting the oncoming stench.

"Damn, why do ether repositories always smell so awful?" Petra asked. She held her nose tight and tried to push through the nauseous smell, not that she had a choice.

Inside were hundreds of canisters that looked like large test tubes. They were empty except for an opaque, blue liquid. Hundreds of wires ran along the floor and ceiling, and piles of soul stones littered the ground, though devoid of any light.

"Looks like they managed to clean us right out," Marco observed. He headed for a table in the middle of the room and picked up a few pieces of paper. "This is gonna take weeks to replace. Well, that sucks."

"We went through all the trouble of collecting soul stones and sucking the life out of them just to have our army cut down by a watered-down Arch Angel, an annoyingly cheery kid, and a dramatic Ursula. What a waste of time. I don't suppose we can go back to Engvall and take more, can we?"

"I highly doubt it. We cleaned them right out the first time. Even so, the boss should still be pleased with what we've learned. Come on—I think it's time we made a little stop by the control room."

The control room was located at the front of Leviathan. It was the biggest room in the ship, with an octagonal shape and a balcony wrapping around its edge. On the front walls, a bunch of screens displayed the areas around the ship. The outside view for navigation was the most prominent screen, but there were also smaller screens that hovered on the wall, like projections showing their surroundings. In the middle of the room was a table taking up much of the ground-floor space. A scale model of Alterra was currently being projected, though it could easily be used for many other things as well.

"Hey, Oberon, we're back," Petra hollered as the door below the balcony slid open. She and Marco strode through to see two Angels, both male, in the room. One of them stood waving his hand as he maneuvered around the different skeletal terrains of the Alterra map. He was tall and lean, but his body was sculpted with muscles. He wore all black with trims of gold and purple around his collar, while his hair was spiked with a bandana. Reflected through his eyes was an Angel completely void of emotion. On his back were two swords, crossing to make an X. He paid no mind to Petra's noisy entrance, continuing instead with his work.

Standing on the balcony grazing over the screens was the second man. He turned around to acknowledge his subordinates' appearance. Unlike the other male Angel, this one was quite a bit scrawnier. He had a sweet face, one that would make people smile, which was something he often did himself. The armour around his body was white and gold, and a magnificent sword hung at his side. He gave them a wave and hopped over the balcony, his white cape flapping as he landed.

"Welcome back, you two. And might I say, you did a splendid job—far more than I was expecting." The way he spoke was nothing like how a tyrant Angel would sound. His voice was far softer and carried no malice whatsoever. He smiled at them, displaying a proud face of confidence.

"Thanks, but it would've been much better if the Arch Angel had come with us. We knew it wouldn't be easy, though," Marco said.

The Angel who continued circling the map finally spoke, his voice ice cold. "As long as she continues to harbour only a fraction of her power, she is currently of no use to us anyway."

"Now now, Gabriel—there's no need for such a pessimistic attitude." There was a cocky snarl in Oberon's voice. "Our dear Arch Angel has only just returned to us. She will need time to regain the power she used in the Angel Wars. It's only right that we give her that time."

"Wait," Petra cut in. "If you already knew all this, then why'd you send us down there in the first place? We wasted all the cloned Angels we'd stored up trying to take her by force!"

Oberon headed back toward the display map in the middle of the room. "Those Angels were nothing but fodder. A simple concoction of concentrated ether mixed with a dead soul stone. The real reason I sent you down was so that we could set the Arch Angel on the correct path. Her memories are gone, and anyone placed in that position would desire to get them back. Memories, after all, are what continue to make life worth living. But history does not have fond memories of her, and I knew that would be a deterrent. If she were to abandon finding her memories, then she'd never gain back her true power. And I simply can't have that."

"Well, aren't *you* perceptive?" Marco sneered. "And what about the boy? Did you see that one coming?"

"No. I must admit that when the Arch Angel pumped him full of ether, I expected him to die," Oberon said. "For a mortal, that power should've been enough to end him. But it would appear that he's taken a shining to the Arch Angel. His heart is in a good place, though, and I believe he'll be more than suitable for this journey."

A light flashed in the center of the room and the map started to zoom in on its destination. The terrain was bumpy and filled with mountains, but making out distinct features was impossible due to the wireframe nature of the map.

"Oberon, I've found what you're looking for," Gabriel said.

Oberon hurried over to the map, then typed away on a nearby computer. "Wonderful. Excellent work, Gabriel."

"And where exactly is it that we're planning on going?" Petra asked.

Oberon laughed and jumped up to the balcony. "That's easy. We're going to find The Guardian Angel."

AFTERWARD

Hi, this is William Richards, author of *Guardian Angels*. I hope you enjoyed the start of this new series. Now that the book is finished, I wanted to take a moment to talk to you, the reader.

First, I want to say thank you for taking the time to read my work. It means the world to me. I love to write, and tell stories, and if I can bring a little bit of joy and entertainment to you in the process, then I suppose I've done my job.

I've always wondered what it would be like to write a more fantasy heavy book, with magic, and swords, and other aspects that ignore the everyday mundane. Though there are some similarities to my other series, Elements, I did my best to create new and fresh characters as well. I must say it was a lot of fun to write. Especially Koda the Adventurer, he is certainly one of my all time favourites to write. Of course, I also very much enjoy Noah and Lucia as well, and I hope you do to.

All of that said, I'll finish with this, like always:

Thank you to StalkingP for her continued commitment to working with me, and I love what she did with the main characters! I can't wait to see how her art develops in this series and beyond.

Thanks also to Rob Peace for his care and dedicated focus with the editing process. He has helped elevate my work in so many ways, and also taught me a ton about writing in general.

Thank you to my family and friends for not being the kind of people to tell me to "just give up…nobody reads these books, anyway — who cares?" I appreciate your support immensely.

PLEASE REVIEW

If you enjoyed this book, please consider writing a review on Amazon.com or Kobo.com, Goodreads, or anywhere else. It really helps!